A
VERY BARRIE
CHRISTMAS

a *Poppy Creek*
Novella

USA TODAY BESTSELLING AUTHOR
RACHAEL BLOOME

For film and TV rights: hello@rachaelbloome.com

Cover Design: Ana Grigoriu-Voicu with Books-Design.

Editing: Krista Dapkey

Proofing: Beth Attwood

SERIES READING ORDER

To everyone in need of some Christmas cheer. And maybe a cup of coffee or two.

LETTER FROM THE AUTHOR

Dear Friend,
   I never expected to write this story. I said goodbye to our friends in Poppy Creek while writing book 8 of the series, The Promise in Poppies.

But Frank Barrie had other ideas. He's quite opinionated, as you'll soon see in this story, if you haven't met him already.

I'm so grateful he barged back into my life—grumbles and all—because I've loved spending time with him and Beverly. And, of course, meeting Nate and Juliet, too.

I hope you enjoy this festive romp in the friendliest town on earth. If this is your first trip to Poppy Creek, may it be the first of many.

If you'd like to chat more, you can reach me via email at hello@rachaelbloome.com, through my website, or in my private Facebook group, Rachael Bloome's Secret Garden Book Club.

. . .

RACHAEL BLOOME

UNTIL NEXT TIME,
   Happy Reading!

Rachael Bloome

SPECIAL BONUS OFFER

As a special thank you to my readers, I've created an exclusive (and completely FREE) members-only area of my website called the Secret Garden Club. When you join, you'll receive access to a wealth of bonus content, including short stories, extra scenes, and more.

Oh, and did I mention FREE BOOKS?

Adding to the fun, the content is regularly updated, so you never know what goodies you'll find.

By joining, you'll also receive exclusive emails with writing updates, sneak peeks, sales, freebies, and giveaways.

I'd love to stay in touch. You can join here: www.rachaelbloome.com/pages/secret-garden-club.

CHAPTER 1

FRANK

Frank Barrie liked coffee more than he liked most people.

He knew coffee. How to roast it, blend it, and brew it. Coffee made sense.

People, though? People didn't make a lick of sense. Especially concerning matters of the heart. He should know. He'd turned stark raving mad the day he met his lovely bride, Beverly.

"Ow!" Frank jerked his hand away from the blazing-hot bread pan. Oven mitt! He needed an oven mitt. How long had it been since he'd baked something?

He fumbled through the drawers and cabinets, grumbling to himself. Beverly assured him the organizational system she'd implemented in their snug farmhouse kitchen was the most logical layout, but even after three years of marriage, he wasn't convinced. What was wrong with the way he had it before? Didn't everyone have a kitchen drawer filled with dead batteries and ketchup packets?

Aha! There it is. She'd hidden the oven mitt in the drawer by the stove.

He removed the bread pan from the oven and set it on the counter. *Huh. That doesn't look right.* The fruitcake in the photo in Beverly's cookbook didn't have charred edges and a gooey center, did it?

He squinted at the open book on the counter. The photo on the page blurred into an indiscernible blob. He supposed his fruitcake *could* look like the picture. There was no way to know for sure without putting on his reading glasses. Maybe he should've worn them to read the recipe? Oh, well. It was too late now. He nudged the pan with the oven mitt and the loaf jiggled. *Hmm.* Perhaps he could pass it off as Christmas pudding instead?

"Who am I kidding," Frank muttered, ready to scrap the whole foolhardy idea.

He'd wanted to surprise his wife with a cozy Christmas evening when she returned home from her shift at the library. He'd planned every detail, from her favorite Nat King Cole record to a slice of fruitcake waiting for her on a fancy china plate to the crystal goblet of chilled eggnog. The kind made from scratch, not the congealed glop in the carton.

It was all part of Operation Give Beverly the Best Christmas—the Christmas she deserved but never quite got to experience since she'd married her very own Ebenezer Scrooge.

Well, to be fair, he considered himself a *reformed* Scrooge. He'd spent most of his adult life secluded in his own bitter world, hidden from every reminder of the happiness he'd lost when he went off to war. It had taken years—and the kindhearted community of Poppy Creek—to thaw the frozen barrier around his heart. But even now, as he turned over a new, albeit slightly crusty leaf, he found it difficult to change his ways.

The Grinch's heart may have grown three sizes in a single day, but in his late eighties, Frank found the endeavor a little slow going. Sometimes tedious, if he were honest.

But Bevy had put up with his bah-humbugs for long enough. The last few years, he'd tried to go along with her holiday shenanigans, but not without a grumble or two. Or six or seven.

Not this year, though. This year, he was a whole new man. Like good ole Ebenezer, post haunting. Although, so far, he wasn't off to a great start.

He glowered at the offending fruitcake, as if it had purposefully plotted against him. What would it take to conjure a couple of Christmas ghosts to help him make a festive fruitcake? It was the first day in December, and he'd already failed. How could he give his wife the perfect Christmas when his personality seemed to repel all things merry and bright?

He needed a cup of coffee.

Maybe two.

He poured velvety arabica beans into the burr grinder, admiring their deep chocolatey-brown hue. He may not be able to bake a fruitcake to save his life, but he could still roast the best cup of coffee on the West Coast. Probably both coasts and every state in between, but he didn't want to brag.

The metal gears of the grinder emanated a pleasant

whirring sound, followed by the crackle of crunching beans. A much more enjoyable melody than any rendition of "Jingle Bells" he'd ever heard.

Eyes closed, he inhaled the earthy aroma, already feeling a sense of calm slip over him.

Then the phone rang, and the shrill squawk cut through his brief moment of serenity.

Frank groaned.

The grinder rumbled to a stop.

He glanced longingly at his French press, and the phone screeched again.

"Hold your horses," he grumbled, shuffling toward the landline secured to the wall. *This better be important.*

"What?" he barked into the receiver, not one for pleasantries.

"Hi, Mr. Barrie!" The unnaturally chipper contralto of Susan Hiesman filled the speaker. The director of Forgotten Heroes, a veterans' homeless shelter in San Francisco, called Frank frequently, but he still wasn't used to her inhuman energy levels. He suspected that out of all the coffee he donated to the shelter, she consumed more than half of it.

"Hi, Susan. Are you out of coffee already?" His roasting apprentice, Vick Johnson, had just delivered fifty pounds last week.

"No, no. It's not that. Everyone's loving the new blends. Rudolph's Roast! Blitzen's Brew! So fun and festive!"

"You can blame Vick for those." He'd argued that reindeer didn't drink coffee, and Vick had responded with, "How can you be sure? Maybe coffee is what gives them the ability to fly," to which Frank had merely grunted, admitting defeat. No point in quibbling over the caffeine consumption of air-bound mammals that didn't exist.

"Please tell him they're delightful," Susan chirped. "But I'm not calling about coffee this time."

"How much money do you need?" He was used to cutting a check whenever the shelter needed a cash infusion. Several years ago, he wrote a book called *The Mariposa Method*—his manifesto, chronicling his foray into the world of coffee and the development of his proprietary roasting method—that took off, hitting all kinds of hoity-toity bestseller lists, and subsequently stuffed his bank account with more money than he could ever spend. Especially since he preferred to live a quiet life in a small, rural town with the woman he loved who only ever splurged on books and tea. Tea! Not coffee. Her only flaw.

"Actually, I need a different kind of favor."

Uh-oh. Something in her tone made him nervous. It sounded as if whatever she was about to ask him, she knew he wouldn't like it.

He waited for her to fill the silence.

"There's this young man at the shelter. Private Nathanial Henderson. He stayed with us briefly last year, but now he's a volunteer. He's here almost every day, helping other struggling vets get back on their feet. He's kind-hearted and a hard worker. A really upstanding young man."

"Uh-huh," Frank mumbled. The last time he'd received a sales pitch this enthusiastic, some flimflammer had tried to sell him a 1955 Buick Roadmaster with a busted transmission.

"He had a tough time when he left the military," Susan

continued. "He has no family. Aged out of foster care. Mostly group homes. He had no one waiting for him when he got back from Iraq. You know how hard it is when they come home and have no support system."

He did. And he'd made it a personal goal to help out in as many ways as possible.

"Anyway, he's been a godsend at the shelter, and I'd love to find a way to thank him, which got me thinking," Susan rambled on at a mile a millisecond. "He has this fascination with all things Christmas. Probably because he's never really experienced the holidays the way most of us have. It would be so wonderful to give him a real, homey Christmas. Snow. Caroling. Sugar cookies. Quaint small-town events. All the trimmings."

It was a nice idea, but what did it have to do with him?

"I was thinking about all the things Beverly's said about your hometown during the holidays," Susan continued, as if she'd read his thoughts. "Poppy Creek sounds magical. Like a tiny slice of heaven tucked away, right here in Northern California."

Oh, no. The other shoe finally dropped. And it kicked him in the tokus on the way down.

"I was wondering if you and Beverly might let Nate visit you for a few days? Maybe give him a taste of Christmas? He won't be a bother. And you'd be doing something wonderful for a young man who served our country. Be a hero for this hero, Mr. Barrie."

Laying it on a little thick, Susan. Although, she sure knew his weak spots.

But as Susan spouted more of Private Henderson's admirable qualities, every muscle in Frank's body clenched. Invite a stranger into his personal space? And during the holidays? He'd rather get a root canal and a colonoscopy at the same time.

He was about to tell Susan as much, when a thought struck him. Why did her proposition sound so familiar? Hadn't he heard of a similar scenario somewhere else recently?

He furrowed his brow, mentally rummaging through the discombobulated filing cabinet of his memory where reruns of *Jeopardy!* mingled with images of his childhood. The other night, Bevy made him watch *Christmas in Connecticut*—her favorite Christmas movie she watched every year right after she packed up the Thanksgiving leftovers.

He wasn't too keen on sappy holiday romances. Too much faffing about and not enough gunfire. But that Barbara Stanwyck sure was a looker.

Anyway, in the film, Barbara Stanwyck's character invited a war hero to her home to experience the perfect small-town Christmas.

If he couldn't make Bevy an edible fruitcake, maybe he could help her reenact her favorite Christmas movie? Minus the falling in love with the soldier part, obviously.

Every time she watched the film—which she knew by heart—her eyes took on this misty sheen, and she'd murmur something about how wonderful it would be to give someone the gift of Christmas. Personally, he preferred to give practical gifts, like a savings bond. But if Bevy wanted to hand out Christmas cheer, he would help make it happen.

"Mr. Barrie?" Susan said cautiously, as if she'd interpreted his silence as a bad sign. "If it's too inconvenient, I completely under—"

"We'll do it."

"What?" Her surprise echoed through the speaker.

"I said we'll do it. I can't promise snow, but we can handle the sugar cookies and Christmas carols. Except for 'Jingle Bells.' I draw the line at 'Jingle Bells.'"

"Okay. Well. Um. Wow. Are you sure? Do you need to discuss it with Beverly first?"

"No. I'd like to surprise her." For some incomprehensible reason, his wife loved surprises. One of her endearing —and utterly baffling—quirks. In his opinion, *surprise* was simply another way to spell *unnecessary stress*. And he didn't need one more factor contributing to his heartburn.

"Well, uh, great! Thank you. This is incredible news! You're doing a very kind thing. I can't wait to tell Nate! When would you like him to come? And for how long?"

"Send him our way whenever you want. And let's say… a week?"

"Fabulous! This is so exciting." Susan's voice became even higher pitched than usual, which didn't seem possible. "I'll talk to Nate and get back to you with his travel details. But I imagine he'll be eager to come soon. He mentioned his place of employment is closing for a few days to repair a leaky roof. Is it okay if he comes as early as tomorrow?"

"That's fine." Bevy kept the spare room ready for the rare occasion her niece, Juliet, came to visit.

"Oh my goodness! I can't believe it. He'll be ecstatic! I'll tell him the good news as soon as we get off the phone." Susan continued to ramble in her excitement, but Frank barely registered a single word beyond her gushing goodbye and the *click* of the receiver when she finally hung up the phone. He was too busy formulating how he'd unveil the surprise to Bevy.

By THE TIME she returned home later that evening, he'd planned the perfect reveal. He'd made flapjacks for dinner, inspired by one of Bevy's favorite scenes in *Christmas in Connecticut*—and one of the only things he could cook—and had "O Little Town of Bethlehem" playing in the background. A warm fire crackled in the fireplace, casting a cozy glow around the sitting room where he'd arranged two TV tray tables in front of the couch. He lit a candle on the coffee table and waited eagerly.

But when she burst through the front door, shrugging out of her wool coat, she seemed eager to share her own news. "Darling, guess who called me today?" She paused, taking in the festive scene he'd set, her periwinkle-blue eyes shining. "Oh, how lovely! You did all this for me?"

He patted the cushion beside him. "There's more. But first, tell me your news." He didn't want a single distraction when his turn came.

She joined him on the couch, brimming with joyful energy. "Juliet called! And she wants to come for a visit. Isn't that wonderful?"

She positively glowed in her excitement. How did he get so lucky to marry such a beautiful bride?

"That's great, Bevy." His people-loving wife would get to welcome two guests this holiday season. She'd be in hospitality heaven. "When is she coming?"

"That's the best part!" She clasped her hands in delight. "She's arriving tomorrow!"

Uh-oh. Talk about bad timing.

Maybe he could call Susan and cancel? Or reschedule?

His heart sank. She'd probably already told Private Henderson. He hated to go back on his word.

Ugh. Once again, his good intentions had landed him in hot water.

"What's wrong?" Beverly's happy glow faltered. "Is it okay if Juliet visits?"

"Of course. Jules is always welcome here," he assured her, using her niece's nickname to drive home his point. "But there's a... slight snag." *To put it mildly.*

His wife waited expectantly for him to elaborate.

"I just got off the phone with Susan."

"Oh! How's she doing? Is everything okay at the shelter? I've been meaning to send her some sugar cookies."

"Everything's fine. But I—" He hesitated. *Cut to the chase, old man,* he chided himself. *No time to lollygag.* "I agreed to host a young veteran for a few days," he blurted. "We're supposed to give him a taste of a traditional Christmas, like that movie you love. I thought it would be a nice surprise."

"You dear, sweet, thoughtful man." Her delicate features softened with affection, and she gazed at him with a depth of love he still couldn't believe belonged to him. "What a lovely thing to do. I know how much you dislike having company."

"You're not upset it'll overlap with Juliet's visit?"

"Not at all! I'm delighted to have him stay with us. We have plenty of space."

He frowned. *Plenty* seemed like an exaggeration. Their three-bedroom farmhouse had only one guest room.

As if she could read his mind, Bevy said, "We'll make up a bed in your study. It'll be cozy, but that's part of the fun."

Part of the fun? And what was the other part? Foregoing his coveted peace and quiet? Cohabitating with a stranger? And what about Bevy's niece? What would Juliet think about spending the holidays with a man she'd never met? What if they didn't get along?

A sense of dread seeped into his tired bones.

What if this latest fiasco turned out to be even more disastrous than his fruitcake?

CHAPTER 2

NATE

Nate Henderson white-knuckled the steering wheel as the ancient Toyota Camry hit another pothole and the entire chassis rattled as if it might break off in chunks and litter the asphalt.

He was grateful Susan had lent him her extra car, but based on the way it clattered and creaked on the battered country road, he might've been safer taking the bus. Or a bucking bronco.

Rolling his shoulders a few times, he tried to relax. *Remember your resolution, Nate. Focus on the positive.*

Through the dusty, chipped windshield, he admired the thick veil of pine trees on either side of the winding road. He cracked the window, letting in a rush of cold wind that smelled like Christmas. Air that crisp, sweet, and refreshing didn't exist in San Francisco. At least, not in the parts of the city he frequented.

He still couldn't believe his luck. When Susan told him he'd be heading to Poppy Creek for a few days to experience the kind of Christmas he'd only ever seen in movies, he'd made her repeat herself three times. Random acts of awesomeness didn't happen to guys like him.

The Camry's engine stuttered, and smoke spilled from the hood.

Great. Guess his dose of good luck just ran out.

He coasted toward the side of the road, stalling in a patch of dirt. The car's engine released a shuddering sigh, as if thankful for a chance to rest. "Don't worry, old girl. You did your best." Nate patted the dash before he climbed out of the driver's seat.

What now? He doubted looking under the hood would do any good. Susan didn't own a tool kit, even if the car stood a fighting chance, which it clearly didn't.

He lugged his duffel bag out of the back seat, then grabbed the bouquet of red and white carnations from the footwell. He'd wanted to give Beverly roses as a token of thanks for her hospitality, but he couldn't afford them on his piddly salary as a part-time security guard. At least the carnations looked festive.

Nestling the flowers on top of the duffel, he slung the bag over his shoulder. *Time to walk.* It would be nightfall in a few hours. And according to the sign he spotted a ways back, Poppy Creek was still a ten-mile trek. Far, but doable.

The biting breeze cut through his thin coat, and he shivered. Tugging the collar tighter around his neck, he glanced at the darkening sky. Gray, ominous clouds swarmed overhead, forecasting an impending storm.

When it rained, it poured. *Literally.*

Thunder cracked in the distance.

"How are you going to put a positive spin on this

scenario, Mr. Bright Side?" he asked himself, his words escaping in a puff of white.

He dug his hand into the front pocket of his jeans, fingering the cool ceramic button that served as a faithful reminder—a token that got him through the tough times. With a deep, determined breath, he braced himself against the wind and headed toward town. At least the walk would get his blood moving and keep him warm. *Hey! Would you look at that! He'd found a silver lining after all. He was getting pretty good at this positive mindset stuff.*

After a quarter mile, the rumble of an approaching vehicle came from behind. Relieved, Nate stopped and stuck out his thumb. No reason to trudge ten miles in the freezing cold—and potential downpour—if he could hitch a ride.

He waited for the car to stop, but the silver Bentley cruised past him, slow enough he could spot the beautiful brunette behind the wheel staring straight ahead with a strained expression he recognized. During his two-week stint living on the streets of San Francisco, he'd witnessed the uncomfortable mix of guilt and forced obliviousness more times than he could count. While he didn't particularly like what the expression represented, he understood the impulse: If people ignored him, they wouldn't have to face the complicated reality of his existence. Or his humanity.

In this case, he was tempted to give the brunette in the Bentley a free pass. As a general rule, he wouldn't advise single women to pick up strange men on the side of the road. But when he glimpsed her large diamond-studded bumper sticker in the glow of her retreating taillights, he suddenly felt a little less understanding.

If he can't pronounce Proust, then cut him loose.

"Clever," he mumbled with a sarcastic eye roll. Even though he knew the correct pronunciation—*proost*—the pretentious rhyme rubbed him the wrong way. He'd rather walk ten miles in the rain than hitch a ride with a snob.

He trekked another quarter mile before he heard a second vehicle coming from behind. The classic Ford pickup with a faded red paint job immediately pulled over.

A guy in his midthirties rolled down the window. "Hey! Is that your Camry back there?"

"Yeah. Apparently, it couldn't handle the mountain roads."

The guy leaned across the bench seat and swung open the passenger door. "Hop in. I'll give you a ride. We can come back for your car tomorrow. It's going to pour buckets any second. Are you headed into town?"

"Yeah. Thanks." Nate hopped inside and set his duffel on his lap as another crackle of thunder echoed above them.

"I'm Luke Davis, by the way." He flicked on his blinker and eased back onto the road with caution, despite being the only vehicle in sight.

"Nate. Nate Henderson. Thanks for the ride."

"No problem. What brings you to Poppy Creek, Nate?"

"I'm staying with some..." Some what? Friends? He'd never even met the Barries before. "I'm staying with Frank and Beverly Barrie for a few days."

Luke smiled. "We love the Barries! Frank's like a grandfather to my wife, Cassie. She's Poppy Creek's mayor and owns the Calendar Café. Best coffee in town, thanks to Frank, roaster extraordinaire. But then, I'm sure you already know that."

Susan had told him Frank supplied all the coffee for the shelter, but had neglected to mention the man roasted it himself. *Impressive.* Especially for a guy in his eighties.

"Are you family?" Luke asked.

"Friend of a friend," he said vaguely and quickly changed the subject. No need to delve into the details. "This is a great truck."

"Thanks. It belonged to my dad. I've been putting one too many miles on it lately. I should really look into getting a separate delivery vehicle."

Luke must've caught his questioning glance because he added, "I own a custom furniture business, and delivery is often included."

"Cool. Must be nice to run your own business."

"It has its perks. I appreciate the flexible schedule. Especially now that I'm a dad." His features melted into a puddle of paternal affection, and Nate felt a familiar knot in the pit of his stomach.

Being a family man had always seemed like an unattainable dream, like winning the lottery or walking on the moon. And when his life fell apart after the military, the dream had slipped even further from reality into complete and utter fantasyland.

Who would want to marry a guy like him?

"So, Nate. What do you do?" Luke asked.

"I'm a security guard for a small jewelry store." He hadn't wanted to carry a gun again—or even a Taser—but it was the only job he could get. He'd never understood the expression *beggars can't be choosers* more in his life.

He refrained from mentioning his veteran status. People always said something awkward like, "Thank you for your service."

"That's cool."

"It pays the bills." *Barely.* "But I don't think it's what I want to do long-term."

"You're what—late twenties?" Luke asked.

"Twenty-seven."

"When I was your age, I was still practicing law. It took me a while to realize I really wanted to make custom furniture. But I don't regret taking the long road to get here. Thanks to my law degree, I met my wife. Now, we have our beautiful daughter, Edie. All those earlier experiences led to where I am today."

Interesting outlook. Nate didn't particularly care for the experiences of his past. Or where he'd wound up in the present. But he clung to the hope that one day, things would change.

He stared out the window, watching the lush, verdant landscape zip by. The scenery looked like a painting depicting the perfect winter evening.

Maybe this trip to Poppy Creek would mark the moment his life finally turned around?

CHAPTER 3

JULIET

J uliet Klein winced as a pudgy raindrop pelted her windshield. Her thoughts darted to the man she'd passed along the road. She wished she could have offered him a ride. She hated to think of him trudging miles in the pouring rain. But what if he was an axe murderer? Or worse? If he damaged the custom leather seats in her mother's Bentley—the Bentley her mother begrudgingly loaned her when she left for Europe—she could add one more failure to the ever-growing list of disappointments.

No, she'd done the right thing. Single women shouldn't pick up random men on the side of the road. Wasn't that part of the safety course they taught at Reclaim? She'd worked for the nonprofit that helped victims of domestic violence and human trafficking for over five years. She should practice what she preached. Even if she couldn't shake the twinge of guilt. Especially in light of the sudden downpour.

Maybe she could tell Frank when she got to the house,

and he could give the man a ride? That is, if someone else hadn't already stopped to help him. Someone else would stop, wouldn't they?

The rain fell harder, pummeling the roof with an unrelenting percussion. Her stomach sank with the weight of added guilt. The poor guy would be soaked by now. *Ugh.* She didn't need a crippling conscience on top of her debilitating stress. The first ten chapters of her debut novel were due the day after Christmas, and she hadn't made it past the first page.

Okay, she hadn't even made it past the first *paragraph.*

At least, not with anything that would please her editor. The words that easily flowed onto the page were fluffy and fun—words that made her smile. Not deep, profound prose worthy of a Pulitzer.

Why had she promised her editor *A Christmas Carol* for the twenty-first century? Something deserving of the *New York Times* Best Sellers list that all the critics would adore. With all her overselling, she'd jinxed herself, making it impossible to string two words together let alone pen a masterpiece for the modern day.

Her windshield wipers swished, clearing the curtain of water just long enough for her to glimpse the moss-green farmhouse at the end of the gravel lane. The amber glow of a lamp in the front window welcomed her.

How long had it been since she'd visited Aunt Beverly? *Too long.* She'd forgotten how much she loved it here, away from the bright lights and frenetic energy of San Francisco. When she was younger, she couldn't wait to venture to the big city, believing the poet Ezra Pound when he said "all great art is born of the metropolis." But now, at twenty-six, she wondered if Henry David Thoreau had it right when he said "city life is millions of people being lonesome together."

She loved her job as a media and marketing manager at Reclaim, but she often worked from home. Even with two roommates crammed into a tiny two-bedroom apartment, she spent most of her time alone. When was her last date? *Oh, yeah.* Almost three months ago. The guy had spent the entire meal extolling the impeccable pedigree of his teacup Maltese. She was convinced he would've rather brought his dog to dinner than her, if the Michelin-star restaurant had allowed pets.

Dismissing the unpleasant memory, she parked as close to the house as possible without blocking the front steps. Abandoning her suitcase in the trunk for later, she grabbed her overnight bag and sprinted from the car to the safety of the porch. Shivering on the stoop, she rang the doorbell and waited.

"My heavens, child. Come in, come in." Her aunt wrapped an arm around her waist, ushering her inside like a mother hen shielding her baby chick beneath her wing.

As soon as Juliet crossed the threshold, the warmth of a blazing fire enveloped her, along with the enticing aroma of freshly baked gingerbread. A fragrant cedar garland decorated the rough-hewn mantel, dotted with flickering candles and a porcelain nativity set.

She'd been so busy stressing over her deadline, she hadn't had the time or energy to decorate. And her room-mates—a flight attendant and a nightclub DJ who both slept most of the day—considered one strand of twinkle lights and a disco ball satisfactory decor. She'd convinced herself she didn't care, but now, taking in her aunt's beautiful adornments, she realized how much she missed the festive touches. "Aunt Beverly, your home looks amazing."

"Thank you, sweetheart. How was the drive?" Her aunt helped her out of her coat and hung it on the vintage hall stand.

"Uneventful." *Except for the poor hitchhiker I left stranded on the side of the road*, she thought with another pang of guilt. "Is Frank home?" With his bad eyesight—and refusal to wear his glasses—it probably wasn't wise to send him out in the storm alone. But she could drive and bring Frank along for backup.

"He's in the kitchen. As soon as he saw your headlights coming down the drive, he went to make a fresh pot of coffee. Figured you could use some warming up."

"How thoughtful." Juliet smiled. Her uncle-in-law could be a little cranky—or downright ornery sometimes—but she'd quickly learned that he had a soft, gooey center beneath his crusty exterior.

"How's your book coming along, dear?" Aunt Beverly led her into the sitting room, situating her in a plump armchair closest to the fire.

"Swimmingly," she lied. How could she tell her aunt the truth? In her family, the ink in their veins ran thicker than blood. Her father was a well-respected poet, and her mother was a prestigious English lit professor on a teaching fellowship at Oxford. Aunt Beverly was a head librarian. And even Frank, the newest member of the family, had written two best-selling nonfiction titles—*The Mariposa Method* and the sequel, *The Mariposa Method: Expanded.*

How could she admit that she was about to blow her first big break? The big break her mother secured by calling in every favor from every single contact she had. She couldn't let everyone down. She'd simply have to find a way to write the hit novel she'd promised.

"I can't thank you and Frank enough for letting me stay with you during the holidays. A quiet writing retreat away from the noise and distraction of the city is exactly what I need to finish the last few pages." If by *the last few*, she meant all ten chapters.

"We're delighted to have you. But there is one minor change I need to tell you about."

"Oh?"

"Before Frank knew you were coming, he agreed to host a young man from Forgotten Heroes, the veterans' homeless shelter that Frank's supported for years."

"Oh," Juliet repeated, her heart sinking. She adored Frank's altruism, but the timing couldn't be worse. *Stop being so selfish, Juliet. It'll be fine.* "That's so kind of you both. And definitely not a problem. I'll mostly keep to myself, anyway."

"I knew you wouldn't mind. And you can have the guest room. I've made up a bed for Private Henderson in Frank's study."

Private Henderson... I wonder what he's like?

Most of the homeless men she encountered were a little rough around the edges. Some had serious issues with substance abuse or mental illness. Others had experienced a series of unfortunate events outside their control.

What was this soldier's story? And how would she ensure he wasn't a distraction from her writing?

"Actually, Aunt Beverly," she said as an idea struck her, "would you mind if I stay in the study instead?"

"Not at all, dear. But what makes you ask? The spare room is much more comfortable."

"I like the ambiance of the study. I think being surrounded by Frank's old books and his antique typewriter will lend some writerly inspiration."

Beverly smiled. "You writers and your quirky superstitions. Whatever helps."

"Thanks. When is your other guest supposed to arrive?" Hopefully she'd get a few days of solitude first.

"Any minute now."

Darn. "What do you know about him?"

"Not much. But he sounds like a lovely young man who's had a bit of bad luck. He's staying with us to experience an authentic small-town Christmas. Believe it or not, the poor boy has never really celebrated the holidays."

"So, it's kinda like Make a Wish: Christmas Edition?"

"Something like that."

Interesting. Juliet's mind spun with a myriad of thoughts. Maybe there was a story idea in there somewhere?

Before she could give any more thought to a plot line, the doorbell rang.

"Oh! That must be him right now." Brightening, Beverly padded to the front door.

Juliet held her breath expectantly. What if her aunt's new houseguest proved to be the spark of inspiration she needed?

She suppressed a sigh of disappointment when Luke Davis's tall, broad frame filled the doorway. She'd met Luke before, during her previous visits to Poppy Creek.

And she'd heard wonderful things about his wife and the town's new mayor, Cassie. But neither Luke nor Cassie could help her solve the problem of her missing plot.

"Hi, Beverly." Luke pushed his damp dark hair off his forehead.

"Luke, what a nice surprise! What brings you by in this unpleasant weather?"

"Your friend Nate had a bit of car trouble, so I gave him a ride." Luke stepped aside, revealing the man standing behind him.

Juliet's heartbeat faltered and heat crept up her neck.

Although she'd caught only a glimpse of him earlier, she recognized the man's pin-straight posture and the duffel bag draped over his shoulder.

And from the look of his furrowed brow, he recognized her, too.

Of all the men in the world, why did her aunt's guest have to be the one she'd left stranded on the side of the road?

CHAPTER 4

NATE

W*ell, this is uncomfortable.*

Nate wished Luke didn't have to hurry home to his family. He needed another buffer between him and the brunette in the Bentley.

"Nathaniel, welcome!" The older lady with long silvery hair wrapped in a bun on top of her head gathered him in a warm, motherly hug.

He wasn't sure what to do, so he patted her back awkwardly. "Please, call me Nate."

"Nate." She stepped back and smiled brightly. "I'm Beverly. And this is my husband, Frank."

Frank grunted an indiscernible greeting, but gave him a firm, semifriendly handshake. Nate didn't mind a man of few words. And from what Susan said, more than half of Frank's vocabulary consisted of blunt statements and gruff sarcasm. So, silence and a solid handshake seemed like a decent start.

"It's a pleasure to meet you both. Thank you for

welcoming me into your home." He retrieved the bouquet from on top of the duffel bag. "These are for you."

"Oh, how lovely! Carnations are my favorite. Thank you! A gift really wasn't necessary. We're delighted to have you," Beverly said with a soft, sincere tone. She struck him as the sort of person who would struggle to say an unkind word about anyone. "This is my niece, Juliet. Although her friends call her Jules."

"Nice to meet you, Juliet." He hoped his choice of address wasn't perceived as a slight, but they definitely weren't friends.

"Nice to meet you, too." Miss Proust—who wore a coat that looked like cashmere and pearls that would probably go for over five grand at the jewelry store where he worked—wouldn't meet his eye, and she shifted her feet as if she couldn't wait to sprint from the room.

What had Frank and Beverly told Juliet about him? Did she know he'd spent some time living on the streets? Even now, he wasn't exactly high-class. He worked part-time, volunteered the rest of the week, and lived in a studio apartment above a greasy pizza joint. Most of his belongings smelled like pepperoni and stale garlic bread. Was she averse to associate with someone of his lowly social status? The lyrics to one of *Aladdin*'s opening songs echoed in his mind, particularly the part about riffraff and street rats.

"Juliet is a novelist," Beverly said proudly.

Well, that explained the Proust bumper sticker. From the looks of her expensive outfit, she did quite well for herself, too. "Nice. Anything I've read?"

"No." Juliet's gaze briefly flitted to his face, then back to the floor.

She probably figured he was too uncultured to read. He smiled to himself, thinking about the worn copies of *White Fang* and *West-Running Brook* in his duffel bag. Or maybe she wrote romance and made an assumption about his reading preferences based on his gender. "What genre do you write? Contemporary? Regency? Romantasy? Amish?" He rattled off some of the romance subgenres he knew, adding, "Billionaire?" Yeah, that seemed like her vibe.

Her dark doelike eyes narrowed. "Literary fiction, actually."

Shoot. That should've been his first guess. Now he'd offended her by jumping to his own hasty conclusions. *Way to go, Nate.* "Cool. I like the occasional lit fic. I recently read and enjoyed *Remarkably Bright Creatures*," he offered, hoping to find some common ground. "I was pleasantly surprised because magical realism isn't usually my jam." Although an excellent book, he could've done without the coarse language sprinkled throughout. He'd heard more than enough in the military, and preferred to avoid it whenever possible. With contemporary novels, he didn't always know what to expect. One reason he often stuck to the classics.

Her frown lines softened. "I enjoyed that one, as well." She tilted her head, studying him like some oddity she discovered in a novelty shop.

He stared back, trying not to fixate on how attractive he found her impossibly long eyelashes and her wavy brown hair with streaks of caramel woven throughout.

"You're a soldier?"

"Yes, ma'am. Two tours in Iraq."

"What was that like?"

"Hot."

The frown lines on her forehead returned, as if she'd anticipated a juicier response. The only thing he liked less than snobbery was a morbid fascination with war. He'd met countless people who wanted to hear all the gory details without ever leaving the comfort of their cushy recliner.

"Are you hungry?" Beverly quickly redirected the conversation. "There's leftover roast beef in the fridge. I could whip you up a plate. And there's fresh coffee and gingerbread cookies."

"Coffee would be nice. Thanks." He was starving, but didn't want to impose too much right out of the gate. These people had invited him into their home for a week, and he hoped to find ways to be a blessing, not a burden.

"How do you take it?" Beverly asked.

"Black, please."

Frank grunted at his response, and it soundly awfully close to a grunt of approval.

"Wonderful. I'll put these beautiful flowers in some water, then I'll be back with coffee and cookies in a jiffy. Make yourself comfortable." She gestured toward the cozy seating arrangement around the fireplace—a well-worn, plaid couch, matching love seat, and twin armchairs.

"Thanks. Where should I..." He trailed off, tapping a hand to his duffel bag to finish his question.

"Oh! Silly me. You'll want to settle in first." Beverly turned to Juliet. "Be a dear and show Nate to the guest room."

Juliet's eyes widened, and for a second, he thought she might refuse.

"Of course." She offered him a stiff smile, then led him down the hall.

The first door they passed revealed an office lined with floor-to-ceiling bookcases overflowing with old leather-bound books and thick hardbacks. It took all of Nate's self-control not to ditch the tour right then and there in favor of perusing the well-stocked shelves.

They passed the hall bath next. "I guess we'll be sharing this bathroom," Juliet said and quickly showed him where Beverly kept the soaps and towels.

"And this is your room." She opened the door to a small bedroom painted a soothing sage-green color. A large bay window with a built-in seat overlooked a neighboring forest of mature pines and cedar trees. The bed appeared slightly smaller than a queen—maybe a full?—and was piled high with the softest-looking quilts. He didn't even care that the pattern on the topmost quilt featured pink and white roses. If he wasn't so eager to soak up all things Christmas, he'd be tempted to stay in bed the entire week. He might actually get some sleep in a setup that luxurious.

He set his bag on the antique steamer trunk at the foot of the bed, but a nagging suspicion tugged on the back of his mind. "How many guest rooms do they have?" If he had to guess, the farmhouse looked like a three-bedroom, two-bath floor plan.

"Just one."

That's what he thought. He cast a sideways glance at the enticing mound of blankets. *Keep your mouth shut, Nate. Those plump pillows have your name written all over them.* He wanted to take his own advice but couldn't curb his chivalrous impulse. "Then you should have it."

She blinked, taken aback. "Oh. Thank you. That's very kind. But there's a comfortable roll-a-way bed in the study. I actually requested that room. I thought all the books and Frank's old typewriter might be..." She hesitated, as if searching for the right word, before adding, "Motivating."

He nodded. "That makes sense."

They stood, staring at each other again, as if neither one of them knew what to say next.

Nate found his mind wandering, mentally tracing her graceful features. She had this one long tendril that framed the right side of her face. It twisted like a curlicue, and for one wildly inappropriate—admittedly ludicrous—second, he was tempted to wind it around his finger.

He cleared his throat, shoving the unwelcome thought aside. "Should we head back to the living room?"

Juliet jolted out of her own trance. What had she been thinking? Was she appraising his appearance, too? For some reason, he wished he'd shaved that morning.

"Actually, I'm going to grab some coffee and hole up in the study for a while. I'm on a tight deadline."

"Sure." He followed her out of the room, confused by the faint pang of disappointment. Did he actually *want* to spend time with this woman? A woman who openly judged others for their inability to properly pronounce the last name of a French novelist? He hated to admit he found her intriguing and attributed her allure to their shared love of literature. He'd always been a sucker for a pretty girl with a book.

Remember, Nate. The prettiest face in the world can't make up for a bad personality. Even if she is well-read.

His gaze lingered on the gentle swish of her silky hair grazing her shoulders as she walked.

Despite her less-than-stellar first impression, Beverly's niece might be the most beautiful woman he'd ever seen. And based on the way his pulse spiked in her presence, he'd be wise to avoid her at all costs.

Luckily, even if he forgot the whole personality-over-appearance equation, there was zero chance she'd be interested in a barely-making-ends-meet veteran, even if he *could* correctly pronounce Proust.

Plus, there was the not-so-small matter of his past.

If the absence of an impressive paycheck and mailing address didn't scare her off, revealing his darkest, most shameful secret would do the trick.

CHAPTER 5

JULIET

Juliet set her laptop on the small desk by the window and flicked on the floor lamp. A warm glow flooded the room, illuminating worn leather bindings in muted hues of chocolate brown, navy blue, and dark plum. Coupled with the soothing thrum of rain, Frank's study served as the idyllic setting for writerly inspiration. And yet, as Juliet stared at the blank screen, her thoughts weren't alive with character and prose. She couldn't stop thinking about her conversation with Nate.

Why had she blurted "no" so hastily when he'd asked if she'd written anything he might've read? Especially without clarifying. She should've said, "No, I haven't been published yet. I'm working on my debut, but every idea I have reeks of desperation."

Now, he probably thought she'd written him off as a literary Neanderthal. Although, to be fair, most men, in her limited dating experience, didn't read all that much. In fact, on one of her more abysmal dates, the guy had actually told her to give up her author aspirations because in five years or less people would either stop reading altogether or only read books written by artificial intelligence. *What a creep.*

Deep male laughter rumbled from down the hall—Nate's laugh. It was a rich, pleasant sound. But she wasn't sure what to make of the man behind the laugh. He'd read *Remarkably Bright Creatures*, which earned him a check mark in the pro column. But he'd also assumed she wrote romance based solely on her gender. Definite con.

A sour taste rose in her throat as she recalled her intense reaction to his sexist presumption. Was pegging her as a romance writer really so insulting? Or did she feel defensive for another reason?

Her thoughts flew to the contraband buried in the bottom of her bag. The heartwarming, feel-good, put-a-smile-on-your-face holiday romance about two polar opposites who fell in love beneath twinkling lights and mistletoe. The kind of novel her mother derided for cluttering the shelves of bookstores with useless drivel. Her secret vice.

Her cell phone pinged, indicating a new text message.

Mom. Her ears must have been ringing.

Got to brag about you at a dinner party tonight.

Juliet checked the time, 8 p.m. in California, which meant it was around 4 a.m. in England. *Must've been some party.*

Another text came through before she had a chance to respond.

My daughter, the famous author. Has a nice ring to it, doesn't it?

Not famous yet, she texted back. Not even published yet,

37

she refrained from adding.

It's only a matter of time. You have Klein blood. Have you sent your chapters to Debra yet?

Not yet. I still have a few weeks.

Don't dawdle. You want your novel front of mind before the holidays.

Before the holidays? Yeah, right, Juliet scoffed. She'd be lucky to make her original deadline. No way would she voluntarily turn in her chapters sooner.

I'm working on it.

Good. Proud of you, sweetheart.

Juliet's stomach twisted as she texted her mother good night, knowing she'd been less than forthcoming. But as nauseous as she felt withholding the truth, she couldn't admit her struggles or self-doubts. She needed to maintain the illusion. To fake it until she made it. The cost of failure was too high.

Before the book deal, her mother barely ever spoke to her. Even as a child, Juliet felt more like a nuisance to her parents than a source of pride—an inconvenience that got in the way of their literary genius. Then she'd taken a behind-the-scenes position at a nonprofit, and their opinion of her sank even lower. Such a waste of potential, they'd said.

But now? Now, everything had changed.

For the first time in her life, her parents respected her. They were genuinely proud. And they made an effort to spend time with her, to get to know her.

After years of existing in their shadows, she finally had

a real relationship with her parents. And she'd do anything to hold on to the deeply coveted connection for as long as possible.

Even if it meant relying on a miracle.

CHAPTER 6

NATE

Nate strummed his fingers on the upholstered arm of the wingback chair, concentrating on the crackling logs in the hearth. To keep his mind from wandering to Juliet, tucked away in the study, he tried to conjure small talk with Frank. Tried and failed. The man had mastered a nonverbal language composed entirely of grunts, growls, and grumbles.

Nate breathed a sigh of relief when Beverly returned from the kitchen with a steaming cup of black coffee.

"There you are." She handed him the stoneware mug. The smooth ceramic instantly warmed his hands. "I brought you a few cookies, too, in case you change your mind." With a smile, she set the plate on a small side table. It wobbled with the added weight. "Oh, dear. I keep meaning to ask Luke to take a look at this rickety old thing." She repositioned the plate until the tabletop balanced.

"Looks like a wonky leg," Nate noted with an appraising glance. "I can fix that for you with the proper tools." Turning to Frank, he asked, "Got any sandpaper or a file?"

"Out back, in the shed."

"Oh, you don't need to trouble yourself." Beverly waved a hand. "You sit and relax."

"It's no trouble. It'll take me two minutes." He stood, eager to help out. "Would you mind holding on to this for me?" He passed back the coffee mug.

"Are you sure?" Beverly still didn't look convinced.

"Honestly, I'd love to fix it for you. It's the least I can do for all your hospitality."

"But—"

"Let the boy help, Bevy," Frank interjected, hobbling to his feet. "I'll show you the shed." He lifted the walking stick hanging off the back of his chair and gestured for Nate to tag along.

Nate moved the cookies to the coffee table, grabbed his new project, and followed Frank down the hall into the kitchen. Frank opened the back door, letting in a rush of cold, damp air and the loud rumble of raindrops. "You'll find everything you need in there." He pointed to an unassuming toolshed situated beside a large refurbished barn. "The shed, not the barn. The barn's where we roast."

"Got it." Nate nodded, making a mental note to ask Frank for a tour of his roasting process at some point during his stay.

"There's a light switch inside on the right. And here." Frank removed an umbrella off a hook by the door. "Bevy would want me to give you this, even though a little rain never hurt anyone."

Nate grinned. "I can make a run for it."

Frank gave the same grunt of approval Nate heard when he'd asked for his coffee black and returned the umbrella to its resting place.

"I'll be back soon." With the table snug in his grasp, Nate darted down the porch steps, across the yard, and into the shed. He flipped on the light. A single overhead bulb flickered to life.

Raindrops tapped against the shingled roof as he searched for the proper supplies. Once he found a block plane and some sandpaper, he set to work, accompanied by the pleasant acoustics. Did Juliet enjoy writing in the rain? He imagined she did and pictured her typing away in the cozy ambiance of Frank's study, surrounded by books. In his vision, her loose lock of hair fell across her face while she typed, and she gently brushed it aside before returning to her task, her graceful fingers flying across the keys.

Ugh. He had it bad. He needed to think about something else before his imagination got carried away. Determined to push all thoughts of Juliet out his mind, he slid out his phone and dialed the shelter. While it rang, he settled the cell between his chin and shoulder, sanding down the table leg while he waited.

"Forgotten Heroes." Nate immediately recognized the familiar voice of the fresh-faced staff member who volunteered in addition to a full course load at the College of San Mateo.

"Hey, Trevor. It's Nate. How's it going?"

"Good, man. What's up? Where ya been?"

"Visiting some new friends. Is Dozer around?" He'd dubbed his latest mentee Dozer—short for Bulldozer—because the bulky marine had the sort of broad, muscular build that could bust through a brick wall with minimal effort.

"Yeah, I just saw him in the cafeteria. Hang on." He heard the telltale *clunk* of Trevor setting the phone on the desk, then a few minutes later, another, more gravelly voice filled the speaker.

"Hey."

"Hey, D-man. Just calling to check in." Dozer had been at the shelter for two weeks, struggling to stay sober. "How's that book I loaned you?" He'd passed along *Remarkably Bright Creatures* when he'd finished it, hoping the themes of hope, belonging, and redemption resonated with his downtrodden friend.

"Dude, did you know the main character is an octopus?"

Nate stifled a laugh. "Yeah, I picked up on that."

"I thought it was weird at first, but it's pretty cool, I guess." After a short pause, he asked, "When are you coming back?"

"In a few days. So, don't think you have time to sweet-talk yourself into becoming Hazel's new favorite while I'm gone." They had a running joke that the grandmotherly volunteer who worked the breakfast shift gave Nate extra bacon because she liked him the best.

"Oh, it's already happening. This morning, she spread two scoops of jam on my toast. It won't be long before that extra bacon is all mine."

They bantered for a few more minutes before saying goodbye. Nate hung up the phone, relieved Dozer didn't sound as depressed as usual. He worried about the guy more often than not. In many ways, he reminded Nate of himself before he met Susan.

Setting the table down on the ground, he checked the wobbly leg. *Perfectly balanced*. Pleased with the improvement, he put the tools back where he found them, then braced himself for another sprint through the rain.

He'd call Dozer again in a day or two. He knew better than anyone the importance of having a support system. And when you didn't have one, how dark and desolate the world could become.

CHAPTER 7

FRANK

Later that night, Frank sat in bed with a copy of the detective novel *Black Coffee* propped open on his lap. The soft glow of the bedside lamp illuminated the page, but he wasn't focused on the words.

His beautiful wife emerged from the small en suite bathroom in her long flannel nightgown, her shimmering sterling hair in a loose braid down her back.

He readjusted his reading glances, briefly lamenting the slightly fuzzy outline of her slender form. How did he get so lucky to marry such an angel?

He'd been in love one other time, and losing Edith when he went off to war had led to the darkest period in his life. A period when he'd shut himself off from the world, too afraid to feel anything other than his misery and loneliness.

In a way, he admired Private Henderson for emerging from his own "Dark Night of the Soul" to embrace life and experience all the magic and wonder available to him, even if it meant relying on the kindness of strangers. It took courage to accept someone else's help and hospitality, and the boy did so with an openness and humble gratitude that spoke volumes about his character.

"Nate seems like a lovely young man," Beverly said as she slipped into bed. Beautiful *and* a mind reader; he really had hit the jackpot.

"No complaints so far," Frank offered, not one to be overly verbose with his compliments. He'd appreciated the way Private Henderson had insisted on washing his own dishes after coffee and dessert and how he'd carried in a load of firewood without being asked.

"That's high praise, coming from you." Beverly smiled and reached for her worn copy of *Wives and Daughters* on her nightstand. "I really enjoyed having him around tonight."

Frank had to admit, he hadn't begrudged the boy's company, either. After he fixed the table leg, they watched *Miracle on 34th Street*. Private Henderson helped Bevy string popcorn and cranberry garlands, and the two chatterboxes took turns sharing tidbits about the historical origins of jolly old St. Nick, which meant Frank could sit and watch the film without participating in all the chitchat his wife usually initiated in the evenings. Not that he didn't enjoy the occasional conversation, but he typically ran out of words well before she did.

"He's remarkably well-read," Beverly noted. "He and Juliet have a love of books in common."

Uh-oh. Why did she phrase it like that? "You like books, too, you know," he reminded her.

"Of course, dear. But in case you've forgotten, I'm already taken." The twinkle in her eyes gave him pause.

He didn't like where this conversation was headed. "Don't get any cockamamie ideas," he warned her.

"What's so foolhardy about helping two people find love? They both live in San Francisco. They both love literature. They're kind, compassionate, and care about helping others. Plus, they'd make a beautiful couple."

Frank opened his mouth to object, but Bevy clearly wasn't finished yet.

"I realize Nate is a little rough around the edges," she continued, not letting him get a word in edgewise or in between. "And he's still finding his place in the world. But I've always believed a man's character matters more than his social or financial status."

Frank didn't argue. He liked the kid. What little he knew about him, anyway. But Private Henderson could handle his own love life. "I don't think it's wise to meddle in these matters."

"You say meddling. I see it as lending a helping hand."

"Call it what you want, they didn't seem all that fond of each other. If you insist on *helping*, you'll have your work cut out for you."

That was putting it mildly. From what he could see, Jules hadn't been able to escape to the study fast enough, then hadn't rejoined them for the rest of the evening. And the few moments they had been around each other, they'd appeared uncomfortable, at best.

Bevy waved a dismissive hand. "So they got off on the wrong foot. Nothing a little Christmas magic can't cure."

"I don't know, Bevy. There's giving someone the cold shoulder, and then there's whatever those two were doing. It might take a little more than mistletoe to defrost those two icicles."

"Forgive me, darling, but you took a little warming up yourself."

She had a point. "Fair enough. If you're dead set on this matchmaking scheme of yours, I won't interfere."

"That's all I ask." She unscrewed the top of a plastic prescription bottle and pressed a tiny white pill into his palm.

Frank groaned.

"No grumbling. The doctor said you need to take sleeping pills to help with your insomnia."

"Can't I try listening to those library science lectures you showed me on YouTube? That'll put me to sleep faster than any pill." He hated taking medication. Pills for blood pressure. Pills for heartburn. Pills for cholesterol. He might as well open his own pharmacy.

"Frank Barrie, those lectures are fascinating," Bevy scolded. "And no amount of complaining or negotiating is going to change the doctor's orders." She handed him a glass of water from her nightstand. "Now, you're going to swallow that pill on your own or we're going to do it the hard way."

Frank's eyes widened. His sweet, soft-spoken wife could be quite formidable when it came to the welfare of someone she loved. And he didn't want to know what she meant by "the hard way." He swallowed the pill.

"There. Was that so difficult?" She put the glass back on

the nightstand. "Now you'll be well rested for our first day of matchmaking tomorrow."

He still thought the whole idea was a fool's errand, but if Bevy wanted a Christmas miracle, he'd try his hardest to give her one.

And he knew the perfect person to help.

CHAPTER 8

JULIET

The following morning, Juliet cut into the mound of apple cinnamon pancakes piled on her plate, stealing surreptitious glances at the enigmatic man seated across from her. If she'd spotted him somewhere commonplace like a coffee shop or grocery store, she might have secretly checked him out. He had strong, handsome features framed by a sexy five-o'clock shadow. A fit, muscular body that looked insanely attractive in his simple Henley sweater. And those eyes—a striking slate blue that bordered on smoky gray whenever he was deep in thought. Like right now. What exactly did he find so fascinating about the back of the syrup bottle?

She took a bite of pancake, relishing the sweet and spicy flavor notes and plump, airy texture. Her aunt Beverly sure knew how to cook. "Aren't these the best pancakes you've ever tasted?" she asked Nate, then immediately regretted her choice of small talk. Did that sound rude? Like she was implying that because he was homeless he'd never eaten good pancakes before? *Ugh.* What was wrong with her?

Working at Reclaim, she met countless women in similar situations to Nate, and she'd never struggled to connect before. What was it about this man that made her so flustered?

He shot her a strange—possibly offended—look, then said, "They're delicious. Thank you, Mrs. Barrie."

"Please, call me Beverly." Her aunt smiled warmly as she leaned over to refill his coffee. Topping off Juliet's mug next, she asked, "How did the writing go last night, dear?"

"Great," she lied, which was becoming a bad habit. In truth, she'd stared at the blinking cursor until her eyes hurt, then went to bed. While she slept, she dreamt three ghosts had come to visit her. But instead of illuminating her past, present, and future, à la Ebenezer Scrooge, they all revealed the same destiny: her epic failure as a writer. In the final vision before she jolted awake, her parents recoiled in shame while Charles Dickens himself declared her work insipid and banal.

"That's wonderful news," Aunt Beverly chirped, yanking her back to reality. "Then you have time to do me a quick favor this morning?"

"Uh, sure." *That's what you get for fibbing, Jules.*

"Luke came by this morning to let us know he had Nate's car towed to the mechanic, and I asked if we could borrow his truck to transport a Christmas tree. Would you two mind picking one out today?"

"Um." Juliet glanced at Nate, who'd frozen midbite, his eyes wide with a flicker of panic. Why did he seem so perturbed by the proposition? Wasn't the whole point of his visit to maximize the holiday experience? It didn't get much more Christmassy than cutting down your own tree. Or was it the idea of doing it with *her* that bothered him?

From the moment they met, she'd gotten the sense he didn't like her all that much. To be fair, she *had* left him stranded on the side of the road in a rainstorm. But not without a valid reason. Once she had an opportunity to explain and apologize, she could clear the air.

She wasn't sure why his disapproval sat so heavy on her heart. Perhaps because, even in a short amount of time, he seemed like a stand-up guy. Before breakfast, Aunt Beverly had waxed poetic about all the helpful things he'd done last night, from restocking firewood to fixing her wobbly table. According to her aunt, he deserved some sort of sainthood. While Juliet wouldn't pin a medal on the guy just yet, he did strike her as someone sincere and likable. And, for whatever reason, she was determined to change his poor opinion of her. Maybe they'd have a chance to talk on their Christmas tree errand? That is, *if* he agreed to go with her.

"It would be a huge help," Aunt Beverly continued, laying it on thicker than her pancakes. "Frank won't admit it, but he's no spring chicken anymore. I don't want him lugging around a seven-foot tree with his bad back."

Frank grunted but didn't disagree.

"I'd be happy to help, Mrs.—*er*, Beverly," Nate offered without looking in Juliet's direction. "I can manage on my own, if your niece would like to stay here so she can write."

Juliet glowered. *Your niece?* She was sitting two feet across from him. There were few things more annoying than when someone spoke about her as if she wasn't in the room. Irked, she sat a little straighter and announced, "I don't mind coming along. I could use the break." Break? Who was she kidding? The day had just started, and she hadn't even written two words yet. It was quite possible she'd cut off her nose to spite her face, but she couldn't backpedal now.

She forced a smile as Nate shifted uncomfortably in his seat.

"Wonderful!" Aunt Beverly beamed with delight as if she couldn't be happier. She must be really excited about the Christmas tree. "Then it's all settled. You two can leave right after breakfast."

"I'm ready now," Nate said a little too hastily. Was he trying to ditch her already?

"So am I," she countered, chugging her coffee even though the hot liquid burned her throat.

"Before you go," Frank interjected. "There's one more thing I need you to do. I'd like you to deliver a pound of coffee to the Calendar Café. I have a new blend I want Cassie to try. The café's on the way to the Christmas tree farm, so it shouldn't be too much trouble." If it wouldn't be any trouble, why did Frank look so guilty?

Juliet caught Frank and her aunt exchanging a strange look—the type of surreptitious glance shared by coconspirators. But what exactly were they conspiring about?

"Not a problem," Nate told Frank, with an expression that hinted it was definitely a problem.

He politely cleared his plate and avoided her gaze as they climbed into Luke's truck moments later. Staring straight ahead, he turned on the radio and fiddled with the stations until staticky Christmas carols emanated from the ancient speakers.

They drove in silence for several minutes, following the directions Frank had scribbled on a slip of paper, until Juliet couldn't take it anymore.

"So, Nate," she said as casually as possible, while her heart beat a nervous rhythm, "I've been meaning to apologize about last night. I'm sorry I didn't offer you a ride. I can be a little leery of strangers."

He stole a sideways glance, surprise reflected in his striking blue eyes. His features softened, morphing into the faintest of smiles. "Don't worry about it. You did the right thing. For all you know, I could be a psychopath."

"*Could* be?" She raised both eyebrows. "Present tense?"

He flashed a grin—a genuine and ridiculously adorable grin. "You never know."

"In that case, I could be crazy, too."

"The cute ones usually are," he teased, then instantly flushed, strangling the steering wheel as if mortified by what he'd said.

Had Mr. Cold Shoulder just called her cute? And why had the compliment conjured an odd fluttery feeling in the pit of her stomach?

She didn't have time for romantic entanglements. Especially not with a guy she knew nothing about, other than his connection to a homeless shelter.

Okay, Jules. You apologized and cleared the air. Your people-pleaser impulse can relax now.

She shifted in her seat, and Nate cleared his throat.

Cue the awkward silence again.

As she stared out the window, counting the passing pines, she realized her problem wasn't being disliked by Nate.

Rather, the risk largely rested in liking him more than she should.

CHAPTER 9

NATE

Nate wanted to kick himself, but he needed one foot on the gas pedal. *You don't have to say every stupid thing that pops into your head, numbskull.*

Now, Juliet probably thought he was some chauvinist creep who labeled every beautiful woman crazy. And *cute*? Had he really called her *cute*?

His face felt like molten lava, and he prayed she couldn't see the scorch marks beneath his five-o'clock shadow.

Concentrate on something else. Anything else.

He focused his gaze on the road ahead, grateful when the town center came into view.

Four cobbled streets formed a square around a large grassy lawn shaded by an ancient oak tree. Gold rush–era buildings with a mixture of brick, stone, and shiplap siding lined the walkways, each storefront decorated with glittering lights and garlands. Festive greenery wrapped around vintage-style streetlamps, and colorful bunting stretched across the sidewalks.

Nate blinked. Was this town for real? Or was someone secretly filming a Lifetime movie called *The Most Christmassy Town on Earth*?

"Wow," Juliet breathed beside him. "I remember Poppy Creek being festive, but this is a whole other level. I feel like any minute now, Santa and his elves are going to spill out of the shops."

"I had the same thought," he admitted. "Do you know where the café—" Before he could finish his sentence, he spotted a white brick storefront with bistro tables arranged on a cozy patio outside. Two twinkling Christmas trees flanked the front door, and someone had painted an impressive wintry scene on the wall of windows facing the street. A warm amber glow emanated from inside, inviting passersby out of the cold.

A couple emerged from the café carrying steaming to-go mugs. The man pulled an enormous éclair from a white paper bag and took a generous bite. Nate's mouth watered just thinking about all the freshly brewed coffee and baked goods he'd find inside.

"Too bad we filled up on pancakes," Juliet said as he slid into a parking spot on Main Street. "From what I remember, this place has the best cinnamon rolls."

"I always have room for cinnamon rolls." He flashed a half-cocked grin, hoping they could move on from the embarrassment of his earlier blunder. To his relief, she returned his smile as she climbed out of the passenger seat.

With the pound of coffee in hand, he opened the door to the café for Juliet, then followed her inside.

A flood of tantalizing aromas greeted him, from earthy coffee notes to the sweetness of sugar cookies. Walking into the Calendar Café was like stepping into outstretched arms. The warmth and homeyness wrapped around him like a hug.

"Hi! You must be Nate and Juliet." A pretty woman with long hair the color of nutmeg and the deepest green eyes he'd ever seen waved at them from behind the counter. "I'm Cassie, Luke's other half. Frank said you'd be stopping by with some coffee for me." She must've spotted the bag he was carrying.

"It's nice to meet you." Nate shook her hand across the counter. Her grip was firm but soft. *Wow.* Luke really did have it all. A great job. A kind and beautiful wife. He bet his daughter looked like the Gerber baby. But he didn't begrudge the guy. He liked when good things happened to good people.

After the women exchanged a greeting—which included mutual compliments on Juliet's plaid scarf and Cassie's snow globe–shaped earrings—Nate handed Cassie the pound of coffee.

She beamed, hugging the tan craft bag to her cheek. "It's still warm! Doesn't get much fresher than that, does it? Would you like to try a cup? It's a new blend. I'm thinking of calling it Santa's Secret Stash." She grinned. "It'll make an amazing espresso, if you'd like a cappuccino or latte."

"A cappuccino would be great, thanks."

Cassie offered one to Juliet—who asked for a latte instead—then set to work on an antique espresso machine made of gleaming copper. Her hands moved with skill and precision but also with grace, like a dancer or artist, and she didn't slow down even as she made small talk. "So, Nate. Luke tells me you're visiting Poppy Creek to experience a traditional small-town Christmas. How's it going so far?"

"Great, considering this town is more festive than the North Pole. And we're heading to pick out a Christmas tree after this, which fits my plan to partake in as many holiday activities as possible while I'm here."

Cassie's eyes sparkled as she handed him a to-go cup. "I have something that might help you with that." Reaching beneath the counter, she retrieved a hardbound notebook. The words *Christmas Calendar* stretched across the front in gold lettering. "This is something my grandparents made years ago to help them appreciate all the magic of the holidays. Well, not *this* one specifically. I had copies made so I could share the family tradition." She set the notebook in his hands as though bestowing a priceless treasure.

"What is it?"

"It's a Christmas calendar, which is exactly what it sounds like. It lists a different festive activity for each day in December."

"Sounds fun. Thanks."

"My pleasure." Her eyes sparkled again, as if she knew something he didn't.

Turning back to the espresso machine, she moved on to Juliet's latte.

While they waited, Nate flipped through the Christmas Calendar, looking for the day's task. Decorate the Tree. He'd have to ask Frank and Beverly, but it seemed doable. With a quick scan, he noted a few other activities. Bake a Mince Pie. Watch *It's a Wonderful Life*. Go Ice Skating. The book definitely had some good ideas. A vision of Juliet bundled in a winter coat, floating across the ice flashed through his mind. He slammed the book shut, dispelling the far-too-appealing mental image.

Today was a one-time event. They'd pick out a tree together, but after that, he'd keep his distance.

Cassie handed Juliet her latte, but before they could say their goodbyes, a petite blonde woman barged through a swinging door that led to the kitchen, her dark eyes brimming with distress.

"Help!" she cried. "We have a code red emergency!"

The panic in her voice shot straight to Nate's heart. His pulse spiked, pumping too hard and too fast.

Adrenaline flooded his veins, sweeping through his body like a fire blazing out of control, igniting every battle instinct burned into his DNA.

He straightened, hands coiled, ready for action.

CHAPTER 10

JULIET

Juliet jumped at Eliza Parker's dramatic announcement. The spunky blonde baker sure knew how to make an entrance. As kids, Juliet appreciated and admired Eliza's outgoing, over-the-top personality. She'd made her feel welcome the very first time she'd visited her aunt in Poppy Creek.

But today, she wished Eliza hadn't come on so strong. Poor Nate looked ready to barrel onto the battlefield. His hands balled into fists, and his blue eyes darkened like the ocean at nightfall. She'd never felt safer or more protected, and yet she suspected Eliza's so-called emergency wasn't really an emergency at all.

"What's wrong?" Cassie asked calmly, confirming her suspicions.

"My mom just called with the worst news," Eliza lamented. "The costumes for the Christmas pageant arrived, and instead of Victorian England, they're Elizabethan. *Elizabethan,* Cass. It's a disaster!"

Nate's gaze darted from Eliza to Cassie then back to

Eliza again, clearly confused. His shoulders relaxed slightly, and his fists unclenched.

"The middle school is performing *A Christmas Carol* at the end of the month," Cassie explained.

"The whole play is ruined!" Eliza threw up her hands.

This time, Nate glanced at Juliet with an expression that asked, *Do you understand what's happening?*

She gave him a reassuring smile, bolstered by her familiarity with flamboyant personality types like Eliza's. While her mother rarely showed emotion, her father—the more artistic soul—had quite the theatrical flair. He'd once wept actual tears when a butterfly landed on the tip of his pen during one of his poem-writing sessions. Apparently, the butterfly had given his poem its approval. On another occasion, he'd flown into a state of panic when he received the wrong Moleskine notebook in the mail. Something about the margin size. It had taken her mother twenty minutes to calm him down.

When faced with melodrama, she'd learned it was best to remain calm and offer solutions. "What if you did a reimagining?" she asked.

"What do you mean?" Eliza paused her frantic pacing, her curiosity piqued.

"You could do a mashup of Dickens and Shakespeare," Juliet explained. "You could still perform *A Christmas Carol*, just set it during the sixteenth century."

"Huh. Could we do that?" Eliza frowned, as if she wasn't quite convinced the idea would work.

"Sure! You'd have to make some adjustments to the script to account for the language differences, but you could keep the storyline the same."

"I love it!" Cassie beamed. "It's a unique and fresh take on a classic. It sounds like the perfect solution, don't you think, Eliza?"

Her eyebrows knit deep in thought, Eliza ruminated on the suggestion.

Juliet held her breath, surprisingly invested in the outcome of a children's Christmas pageant she'd probably never even see. Most adaptations of Charles Dickens's masterpiece tried to stick as close to the source material as possible. *A Muppet Christmas Carol*—her favorite film version of the story—had added a narrator, but that was the biggest departure she'd seen. A change in the time period could be interesting. But would Eliza go for it?

"I guess it could work," Eliza said slowly. "But rewriting the script seems like a lot of time and effort. And that's assuming we can find someone who knows how to do it."

"It shouldn't take too long. Maybe a day or two," Juliet offered, then realized her mistake.

Cassie met her gaze, her eyes shimmering and hopeful. "You're a writer, aren't you?"

Uh-oh. Why had she opened her big mouth?

"Yes, but not a playwright. I'm a novelist." *Barely*. Could she even claim that title if she didn't finish her novel?

"Do you think you could make the necessary adjustments to the script for us?" Cassie asked.

"Well…" She hesitated. Yes, technically, she could. But did she have time? She glanced between Cassie and Eliza, who stared at her expectantly, as if the fate of the children's pageant rested entirely on her shoulders. Could she let the kids down?

Suppressing a sigh, she offered them a smile. "Of

course. I'd be happy to do it." As she said the words, she realized tweaking the script *did* sound like a fun project. And much easier than penning her pièce de résistance.

While Cassie and Eliza effused their gratitude, she caught Nate watching her with a spark of curiosity. He looked surprised, but in a good way, as if he'd seen her in a new, positive light. Why did the possibility make her toes tingle?

"What about the sets?" Eliza asked suddenly. "They're all Victorian England. They'll have to be redone." Worry crept into her voice, but Cassie continued to smile calmly.

"I'm sure we can make do with some minor modifications," Cassie assured her. "Luke can get started on them tomorrow. I hate to impose during your visit," she said, turning to Nate, "but if you're free, I'm sure Luke would appreciate an extra set of hands."

"I'd be happy to help," Nate offered without hesitation. He really was an upstanding guy.

"Wonderful! Then we'll see you both at the middle school tomorrow. Let's say around 10 a.m.?"

"Both of us?" Juliet asked, unclear why her presence was needed.

"So you can look through the costumes in case you have to make additional character modifications," Cassie explained, her eyes twinkling.

Juliet supposed that made sense. *Maybe.* She stole a glance at Nate.

He stared at the opposite wall, deeply engrossed in reading the chalkboard menu.

So, they'd be spending even more time together tomorrow. The dilemma should fill her with dread. After all, she had a deadline looming. And she very much doubted her editor would accept a Shakespearean rewrite of *A Christmas Carol*, even if it did have more literary clout than the mushy, feel-good stories Juliet devoured—and sometimes scribbled—in private.

Bottom line: she didn't have time to go Christmas tree shopping *or* help with a middle school play. And she certainly didn't have time to be distracted by a man like Nate.

And yet, the more time she spent with him, the more intrigued she became.

CHAPTER 11

NATE

On the drive to the Christmas tree farm, Nate cast a sideways glance at Juliet in the passenger seat, typing away on her phone. How could she be glued to a screen on a day like today? Crisp, clear blue sky sprawled overhead, wiped clean after last night's rain. The scent of damp earth and leaves clung to the air, refreshing and sweet. He could get used to rural, small-town life.

In fact, so far, he loved everything about Poppy Creek. And he couldn't believe his luck back at the coffee shop. He'd actually get to help build the sets for a children's Christmas pageant! What could be more festive than that?

It may even turn out to be an opportunity to spend more time with Juliet. Not that he cared about spending more time with her. Especially if she spent every second on her phone.

After several minutes of driving in silence, they came to a fork in the road. On the right, an elaborate wrought iron archway welcomed them to the Sterling Rose Estate. Dormant flower fields spread out for miles in every direction along with what appeared to be apple trees asleep for the winter.

On the left, a wooden cutout of a reindeer pointed toward a narrow dirt lane. The hand-painted sign underneath read, *Follow me to the Christmas trees.*

Nate veered left and rolled down the window. The invigorating aroma of evergreen flooded the truck, catching Juliet's attention.

She glanced up from her phone. "Wow. That smells incredible."

As she rested the device in her lap, he caught a glimpse of the screen. She appeared to be using some sort of writing app. Working on her novel, maybe?

Although she wrote literary fiction, he couldn't help wondering if her novel featured a romantic subplot. And if so, what kind of romantic hero did she like? Rugged or clean-cut? Alpha or—what did his chatty coworkers call the less dominant guys? Cinnamon rolls? Golden retrievers? Labradoodles? He couldn't remember. Something soft and cuddly. At the very least, Juliet's so-called "book boyfriend" would probably have a full-time job.

Maybe she even had a real living, breathing boyfriend. Why did the possibility spark a pang of disappointment? He pushed the unwanted emotion aside.

As they approached a gravel parking lot, the twangy notes of "Deck the Halls" greeted them, redirecting his wandering thoughts. An elderly gentleman bent over a banjo serenaded two children making s'mores around a large metal-barrel fire pit. The image was right out of an old-timey postcard.

Smiling, Juliet stuffed her phone in the pocket of her

royal-blue peacoat. *Finally.* "I always loved coming here with Aunt Beverly."

"Did you visit often?" He parked beside a big diesel truck and turned off the engine.

"Whenever my parents were busy and didn't want to have a kid around. So, basically, most Christmases until I went away to college."

"Really?" Nate frowned. "Aren't kids supposed to make the holidays more magical?"

"Not when you have prestigious parties to attend." The slam of the passenger door punctuated her statement, but her words sounded more matter-of-fact than bitter. Her nonchalant acceptance of her parents' ambivalence during the holidays made him sad for some reason.

He'd expected to have lonely Christmases growing up in a group home. While most of the staff had cared about him and the other boys and had done their best by them, they had their own lives and families to worry about. The holidays were always the hardest, serving as a blatant reminder that he was on his own. No fun family traditions like he'd seen in the movies. No matching pajamas, hot cocoa by the fire or singing carols together around a slightly out-of-tune piano. He'd grown accustomed to living without a mother's and father's love—without the kind of memories that made Christmas special. But what would it feel like to have two parents in your life who simply chose not to spend the holidays with you?

Oblivious to his melancholy thoughts, Juliet remained focused on the task at hand. "Frank said to get a seven-foot Frazier fir." She led the way toward a row of full, fragrant trees. Their blueish-green branches stretched skyward, revealing a slightly silvery sheen underneath. He'd never seen anything quite like it. But as beautiful as they were, he wasn't ready for the tree shopping experience to be over so quickly.

"First things first." He strode toward the quaint wooden stand offering hot chocolate and s'more supplies.

Juliet begrudgingly followed. "We don't really have time for s'mores."

"Sure we do." He slid a marshmallow onto a roasting stick and passed it to her.

She held the stick at arm's length, as if he'd handed her a live snake.

Nate hid a smile as he made his way to the fire pit. She could use a little Christmas spirit.

The man with the banjo gave a friendly nod without pausing his country-western rendition of "Away in a Manger," and the two kids scooted over to give Nate some room.

With a huff of resignation, Juliet joined him. She stuck her marshmallow directly into the flickering flames as if she couldn't get the ordeal over with fast enough.

The little boy, who appeared to be around six years old, snickered. The girl—presumably his older sister by a few years—jabbed him with her elbow.

"What?" the boy cried. "She's doing it wrong."

Nate suppressed a chuckle, glancing at Juliet to see how she'd react. He expected her to be offended. Or annoyed. Or both.

Instead, she told the boy, "You're right. I'm a little rusty at roasting marshmallows. Do you have any tips?"

He brightened, pleased to be called upon for his expertise. "Sure! You gotta hold it over this part. Watch." He hovered his marshmallow over a patch of smoldering coals and embers. "It takes longer this way, but your marsh-mallow won't get all burnt up."

"That's great advice. Thanks." She followed his lead. "You're really good at this."

"I taught him," his sister interjected, not wanting to be left out.

"Then you're an excellent teacher," Juliet told her, which made the little girl beam with pride.

Nate gawked at the exchange, completely dumb-founded. Miss Proust liked kids? More than that, she was actually good with them. Between agreeing to rewrite the middle school play, and now *this*, she'd thrown him off-balance. Was it possible he'd made one too many assump-tions about her?

They roasted a few more marshmallows, chatting with the kids, who told a funny story about finding a deer mouse in their Christmas tree—that staunchly refused to vacate its cozy home—so they came back with their parents to exchange the tree for one that was rodent-free.

During the lively conversation, Nate tried not to notice how stunning Juliet looked when she smiled, how her dark eyes appeared lit from within. Or how her laughter sounded prettier than a thousand church bells.

Ugh. What a sap. Get ahold of yourself, Nate. You can admire her from afar. But that's all. Got it?

He reiterated the mental pep talk several times as they finished their s'mores and made their way back to the row of Frazier firs. But no matter how adamantly he mentally reinforced the invisible boundary line, he couldn't resist the urge to stick a toe across it. Juliet intrigued him in a way no other woman had. In truth, women and dating had fallen off his radar since he'd joined the military, when every waking moment revolved around the current mission—and making it home alive.

Lost in her own thoughts, Juliet brushed her fingertips across the feathery branches, her expression wistful, almost reverent. "'My woods—the young fir balsams like a place / Where houses all are churches and have spires.'" The familiar words escaped her lips in a soft murmur, and Nate did a double take, certain he'd misheard.

Juliet's eyes widened, and she blushed, as if she'd just realized she'd spoken aloud. "Sorry. The trees made me think of an old poem."

One he knew well. "'I hadn't thought of them as Christmas trees. / I doubt if I was tempted for a moment / To sell them off their feet to go in cars / And leave the slope behind the house all bare, / Where the sun shines now no warmer than the moon.'" He quoted the next few lines of the Robert Frost poem "Christmas Trees"—the poem he'd recently put to memory.

Although not one of Frost's most famous poems, the themes of pure, simple pleasures over consumerism, and the appreciation of country life versus city life, resonated with him on a profound level. It certainly wasn't a poem he'd expected Miss Proust, with her Bentley and pricey pearls, to know by heart.

She met his gaze, equally startled. "You like poetry?"

"Some. Classics, mostly. A lot of the newer stuff doesn't make sense to me. I read one in the *San Francisco Chronicle* the other day about a moldy orange that seemed to be a metaphor for a midlife crisis. By the end of the poem, the orange had become an eagle that somehow laid a dinosaur egg that cracked open, revealing a newly ripened orange. I'd never been more confused in my life."

Cupping a hand to her mouth, Juliet burst into laughter —a deep, boisterous, belly laugh that shook her petite frame.

What had she found so funny? His inability to under-stand the poem? "What?" he asked gruffly, trying not to be offended.

"Sorry, it's just—" She giggled again, then, collecting her breath, she confessed, "My dad wrote that poem."

Oof. Way to go, Nate. He grimaced. "Shoot. I'm sorry. I had no idea."

"It's fine." She gave a don't-even-worry-about-it flick of her hand. "There's no way you could've known. Besides, between you and me, I had no clue what he was talking about, either." She grinned, wiping a tear of laughter from the corner of her eye with her fingertip.

The woman was full of surprises.

"So, your dad's a poet. And you're an author. Quite the literary family."

"*Debut* author, actually. I'm working on my first novel. That's why I said you wouldn't have read anything I'd written."

Ah. That makes sense now. "Gotcha. That's exciting."

"Try terrifying. Your debut sets the tone for your career. There's a lot of pressure to make a big splash right out of the gate, and my editor has particularly lofty expec-tations."

Did he detect doubt in her voice? And why did he have

a sudden urge to put her mind at ease? "I'm sure you have nothing to worry about. If you have an editor, you've already had to prove yourself. They don't hand out publishing contracts to just anybody."

She grimaced. "They do if your father is a famous poet and your mother's a prestigious English lit professor with connections in the publishing world. My editor is a close personal friend of my parents'." Looking embarrassed, Juliet resumed her stroll down the row of trees, brushing their branches with her bare hand as she walked.

"So you had an advantage. That's not necessarily a bad thing. As long as you try your best and make the most of the opportunity."

She paused beside a bushy fir with perfectly shaped branches and met his gaze. "And what if my best isn't good enough?"

Her raw, humble vulnerability rendered him momentarily speechless.

He usually had a knack for pinpointing a person's character within the first fifteen minutes. But when it came to Juliet—and labeling her a shallow, self-absorbed snob—he'd grossly missed the mark. This woman had depth, with real fears and doubts, who genuinely seemed to care about others.

What else had he gotten wrong about her?

CHAPTER 12

Juliet flushed. Why had she bared her deepest fear to a complete stranger? *Ugh.* How embarrassing. Maybe she could redirect the conversation, and they could pretend like it had never happened?

"How about this one?" Quickly turning her back to Nate, she fluffed the branches of the fragrant fir planted directly in front of her. "It's seven feet tall, has sturdy ornament-hanging branches, and I don't see any bald spots."

When he didn't respond, she stole a glance over her shoulder.

Nate studied her, his expression contemplative, as if enmeshed in an internal debate over whether or not to let the previous topic of conversation drop.

Thankfully, he made the right decision. "Sure. It's nice."

"I saw some bow saws hanging on hooks by the entrance. Can you grab one?" she asked, pleased when Nate looked surprised that she knew the proper term for the crescent-shaped saw.

He hesitated a moment, then headed back in the direction they came, leaving her alone to collect herself. Filling her lungs with the crisp, piney air, she shook out her arms and legs, getting the blood flowing again.

Something about Nate made her feel off-balance and unsettled. She usually kept her insecurities tucked tightly away, locked deep inside herself. She never even shared them with previous boyfriends, not wanting to reveal her flaws.

Why bare her soul now? What made Nate so special?

He's not special. You simply feel safe spilling your guts to someone you'll never see again.

Yes, that was the most logical explanation.

You're here for one reason and one reason only, she reminded herself. *To finish the first ten chapters of your novel. Do not, under any circumstances, fall for Private Nathaniel Henderson.*

For one brief moment, she wondered what her parents would say if she dated someone like Nate. Her parents—who cared more about a healthy stock portfolio than someone's personality—would most likely be horrified. Her love life would become one more way she'd sunk below their lofty standards. Not that it mattered. She and Nate were the least likely couple on the planet.

"It's a shame." His deep voice startled her back to reality.

For one unhinged instant, she thought he might be talking about their inauspicious relationship. But he wasn't looking at her. He was staring at the tree, the bow saw grasped tightly in his hand.

"I almost hate to cut it down. It's so—" He paused, as if searching for the right words. "So full of life."

A sharp, penetrating sadness clouded his eyes, transforming the rich blue hue to a muddied gray, as if his thoughts had wandered into murky depths. The intensity of his gaze was almost unnerving.

"Nate?" she prompted gently, but he didn't respond.

He kept staring at the tree, clutching the saw until his knuckles blanched. He'd traveled somewhere deep within himself, somewhere dark and troubling. Where had he gone? What nightmare had his memories forced him to relive?

She wanted to reach for his hand, to pull him to safety. She'd witnessed the relentless effect of trauma too many times to count during her work at Reclaim, watched women struggle to wrench themselves free from the pain of their past.

It wasn't fair that Nate had fulfilled his military duty, and yet, even back home, he could never escape what he'd seen—what he'd done.

For a moment, she couldn't move, mesmerized by the intensity of emotion etched into his face—the deep grooves of grief.

She couldn't fathom the connection between Nate's sudden sadness and cutting down a Christmas tree, but it didn't have to make sense. Her compassion didn't live within the confines of her ability to fully understand. "Actually," she said abruptly, forcing a brightness into her voice. "I changed my mind. I don't want this tree after all."

Her words seemed to snap Nate from his trance. He blinked, glancing left and right, as if his surroundings had suddenly slipped into focus. "What? Why not?" He fixed his gaze on the tree again. "I thought you said it was perfect."

"Perfect is boring. I have a much better idea." Grabbing his free hand, she led him down the next row of trees, following the sign she'd seen earlier, but had casually dismissed. His calloused fingers felt warm against her skin. Strong. Secure. Her heart raced at the intimacy of his touch.

Holding hands was a mistake. A reckless, foolish mistake. A mistake she didn't regret for one second.

She stopped beside a small assortment of potted Christmas trees in various sizes ranging from tabletop trees to giant seven footers, but she didn't let go of his hand. She couldn't, as if the physical contact had cast a spell over her somehow. "Let's get one of these."

"What exactly am I looking at?" He sounded pitchy and out of breath, even though they'd walked only a few feet. Was he thrown off-kilter by their connection, too?

"They're called living Christmas trees." She swallowed, struggling to focus on anything other than the feel of Nate's palm pressed against her own. "You rent them instead of buying. Once you pick the tree you want, you bring it home in the decorative pot, string lights around it, and hang ornaments—just like you would any other tree— then bring it back after the holidays."

"I've never heard of a living Christmas tree." From the clear, sparkling sheen of his eyes, he liked the concept. His grip tightened, ever so slightly, stealing her breath.

Focus, Jules. Inhale, exhale. "It's become trendier over the years. Families can even rent the same tree, year after year, so it can grow along with their children. Isn't that sweet?"

"What happens when the trees outgrow the pot?" His

voice had taken on a raspy quality, and he cleared his throat.

Was holding her hand having an equally disorienting effect on him? For some reason, the innocent gesture suddenly felt like so much more.

"They, uh, get planted in a nearby forest and live a long, full life."

He nodded slowly, as if it took great effort to process her words. "Frank and Beverly won't mind?"

"Not at all. Look. There's a seven-foot Frazier fir in a festive gold pot. Just like Frank ordered. All we have to do is figure out how we'll carry it back to the truck." It had to weigh a hundred pounds.

Her comment drew Nate's attention to their clasped hands. She followed his gaze. Her temperature rose as they stared at their entwined fingers, neither one saying a word, as if a lack of verbal acknowledgment meant they could continue in this state of exhilaration forever. Or was that simply wishful thinking?

"Your girlfriend has excellent taste." A male voice from behind them slammed the world into focus.

Nate yanked his hand away so swiftly it took her a moment to register what happened. And the mortified look on his face hurt far more than it should.

CHAPTER 13

NATE

A guy in his midthirties wearing thick leather gardening gloves glanced between them, grinning at a situation he'd clearly interpreted as a besotted couple buying their first tree together.

Nate burned with embarrassment, as if he'd been caught living in a fantasyland. Holding Juliet's hand had been the best three minutes of his life, but he'd indulged in the moment too long, letting his mind—and *heart*—run wild with impossibilities. Impossibilities like the two of them ever becoming romantically involved.

He needed to set the record straight, but before he had a chance to tell the guy they weren't a couple, the man's face brightened with recognition. "Juliet? Juliet Klein?"

"Reed Hollis!" Juliet beamed. "It's been ages."

"Too long." He pulled Juliet into a side hug, and Nate stiffened, suddenly eyeing him in a new light.

With his thick brown hair and dark eyes, the guy was objectively good-looking, with surprisingly tan skin for the middle of winter. *Aha!* A wedding ring. Nate relaxed as the two continued to chat, then immediately chided himself for being ridiculous.

He had zero future with Juliet. Besides, holding hands had probably meant nothing to her, just a simple, friendly gesture. *Don't blow it out of proportion.*

Despite his rationalizing self-talk, he couldn't shake the feel of her soft skin, or the way their fingers fit so perfectly together. It had been so long since he'd felt that kind of connection, but he knew better than to indulge in a delusion. Why hadn't he let her hand go sooner?

He blamed his weakened emotional state on the implicit flashback triggered by the Christmas tree—or was it the bow saw? Or the loud crackle and pop of the burning logs in the bonfire he'd barely heard on a cognizant level? He still struggled to understand the strange subconscious reactions—the intense feelings unaccompanied by a memory of a specific event—no matter how many times his therapist tried to explain the phenomena to him.

The intangibility of his PTSD, the way it could spring out of nowhere for no obvious reason, is what unnerved him the most. He could battle flesh and blood, but how could he fight something he couldn't see?

At the end of the day, he may never know why he'd reacted the way he did at that moment. But he *did* know, regardless of the reasons, he was grateful to not take another life, even if said life belonged to something as inanimate as a tree. He'd seen too much destruction, too much beauty reduced to rubble. And somehow, it was as if Juliet sensed and understood that in a way no one else had before. At least, no one who hadn't walked a mile in his combat boots.

"I don't think we've seen each other since your senior year of college." Reed's comment dragged Nate from his thoughts, focusing his attention on the guy's conversation with Juliet. "Are you here to spend the holidays with your aunt?"

"Yes, good memory. It's my first time celebrating Christmas with Aunt Beverly since she married Frank. They roped us into getting the tree." She flashed a good-natured grin. "I didn't know you worked here."

"Olivia and I bought the place from Sanders a couple years ago. We merged his acreage with my flower farm next door to create the Sterling Rose Estate. It's a whole operation now. Christmas trees. Flowers. Apple picking. An event center for weddings and other special occasions. We do it all."

"That's amazing. Congratulations."

"Thanks. You, too. I hear you signed an impressive publishing contract."

Juliet blushed, and Nate recalled her confession from moments earlier. Did she really worry her debut novel wouldn't be good enough? And why did he have a strange urge to assure her otherwise?

"I should've known Aunt Beverly would spread the news all over town. But it's not a big deal, honestly."

"It's a huge deal, but I know better than to argue." He grinned, then turned to Nate. "I'm Reed, by the way. Jules and I used to hang out as kids when she'd visit for Christmas and occasionally during the summer."

"Nate." He shook the man's hand. "Nice to meet you."

"Your aunt never mentioned you were dating someone," Reed teased Juliet, eliciting another blush.

"I'm not seeing anyone. Nate and I just met the other day. He's—" She hesitated as if she didn't know how to introduce him.

"I'm staying with Frank and Beverly for the week," he interjected, coming to her rescue. He still wasn't sure how much she knew about him. Except now, she knew he could freeze up over something as ridiculous as a Christmas tree.

"Oh, man. I'm sorry. I just assumed when— You know what? I'm going to stop before I dig the hole any deeper." Reed chuckled. "How 'bout I get a hand truck and help you guys load the tree you picked out?"

"That would be great." Juliet looked relieved to move on from the awkward conversation. "Thanks."

Reed made small talk as they loaded the tree, but Nate couldn't concentrate on anything the guy said.

How could he when Juliet's words still echoed inside his head?

I'm not seeing anyone.

She was single.

There was no logical reason why he should care one way or the other.

After this week, he'd never see her again.

And yet, rational or not, he'd never heard better news in all his life.

CHAPTER 14

FRANK

That evening, Frank couldn't help a satisfied smile as Nate passed Juliet an ornament to hang on the tree. When their fingers grazed, Jules's cheeks flushed, and Nate looked like someone had zapped him with a cattle prod.

Frank wasn't sure what had transpired on their Christmas tree excursion earlier, but Bevy might be onto something with this whole matchmaking thing. And sending them in to see Cassie hadn't been a bad idea, either. Not only had she given Nate the Christmas Calendar—the contents of which would provide a healthy dose of holiday magic—she'd roped them into working on the middle school pageant together.

If he'd learned anything from Bevy's schmaltzy movies, it was that the soon-to-be lovebirds needed an external reason to spend more time together. Oh, and apparently, there's something romantic about airport proposals, which makes about as much sense as stringing pearls on a pig. No one should kneel on a floor that filthy unless they planned to celebrate their engagement with a stomach virus. But he digressed....

Frank glanced at his wife. Beverly flitted around the room, refilling their glasses of eggnog while some peppy song about a Christmas tree farm by a young singer named Taylor Smith—or was it Swift?—bounced around in the background. Juliet had picked the playlist. He would've preferred some Eartha Kitt or Peggy Lee, but the music wasn't terrible. At least it wasn't "Jingle Bells."

As she fussed over her guests, Beverly beamed brighter than the lights on the tree, and Frank allowed himself a few extra seconds of shameless ogling.

Move over, Barbara Stanwyck. You ain't got nothin' on my Bevy.

"A potted Christmas tree is such a lovely idea. Quite ingenious, too." Beverly closed her eyes and inhaled the crisp, tangy scent of pine before hanging her next ornament—a small snowflake made of sea glass.

"Aunt Beverly, that ornament is gorgeous." Peering over her shoulder, Juliet admired the shimmering glass pebbles. Their rainbow palette appeared even more vivid bathed in the glow of the multicolored bulbs. "Where did you get it?"

"Frank bought it during a weekend getaway last year." Bevy cast him a sweet, loving glance. "We went to visit a café that serves his coffee. It's located in the cutest little town called Blessings Bay. We saw the ornament on display in the window and had to get it to commemorate our trip. It's a new tradition we started when we got married. We pick an ornament every Christmas to signify a special memory from that year."

"That's a beautiful tradition," Juliet said with a soft

smile. "You two are so sweet."

Was it his imagination or did Juliet look wistful, as if she wanted the kind of relationship he and Bevy had? If his wife got her Christmas wish, Juliet would be well on her way to happily ever after by New Year's.

"You and Nate should pick out an ornament, too!" Beverly clapped her hands in excitement. "We can go shopping tomorrow."

"Th-the two of us?" Nate stammered, red-faced, as if he'd assumed Bevy meant they should pick out a joint ornament together. To what? Commemorate their blossoming relationship? Frank suppressed a chuckle. Private Henderson must have romance on the brain.

"Of course!" Bevy affirmed. "You can each take one home as a souvenir. A little treat, on me."

"Oh." The boy relaxed at Bevy's clarification. "That's very kind of you."

"I don't know," Juliet interjected. "I wouldn't even know what to pick."

"That's easy, dear! Your ornament should be writing-related, like a book or a pen. To celebrate your big publishing contract."

At Bevy's suggestion, Juliet suddenly focused all her attention on straightening a crooked ornament on the tree. Had something about Bevy's comment made her uncomfortable?

He made a mental note to ask Juliet how the novel was coming along the next time they had a moment alone. He'd written his first book on his own timeline, but he'd been under contract for the second one. And he'd only been able to meet his deadline thanks to Cassie's help.

"Speaking of my big publishing deal"—Juliet smiled, but Frank could tell she'd forced it into existence—"I should get back to work. I have a play to rewrite, too."

"Of course, dear." Bevy hid her disappointment well.

Private Henderson, on the other hand, did not. The young man took a sip of eggnog, but his eyes never left Juliet's face. His gaze followed her out of the room. And if Frank wasn't mistaken, it took all the soldier's self-control not to take off after her.

"What would you choose as your ornament, Nate?" Bevy handed him one end of the popcorn and cranberry garland they'd strung together last night.

"I don't know. Probably a poppy, to signify my time here with all of you." He stretched to start the garland at the top of the tree.

As Frank suspected, Nate's response had melted his wife's heart. She caught Frank's eye and flashed a look that begged, *Can we keep him?* As if the boy were a lost puppy who'd wandered into their yard.

"But they probably don't even make ornaments with poppies on them," Nate added, winding the garland a few loops around the top before passing it back to Beverly.

Before Bevy could respond, the phone wailed from the kitchen.

"I'll get it." Frank shuffled out of his comfy seat on the couch, mentally preparing to let the caller have an earful if they happened to be a solicitor.

"Hello?" he answered in a tone that said, *You'd better have a good reason for calling at this time of night.*

"Hi, Mr. Barrie. It's Susan. How's everything going with Nate's visit?"

"Fine. Why?" The strained timbre of her voice gave him pause. Had she expected something to go wrong?

"No reason. Just wanted to make sure he's settling in okay."

"He seems to be. Want to ask him?"

"No, that's okay. I don't want to bother him."

A long silence lingered on the line, and Frank stared at the receiver. Did Susan have more to say? She didn't seem keen to hang up the phone.

"Everything's fine," Frank offered again, filling the dead air. He thought about adding her car had received a complete tune-up and ran better than ever but figured Nate would want to give her the good news himself. "He's polite and helpful, just like you said. He's decorating the tree with Bevy right now. We haven't had any issues."

Her sigh filled the speaker. "I'm happy to hear it."

Why did she sound so relieved? "Susan, is there something about Private Henderson you're not telling me?"

"Why would you ask that?" she squeaked.

Maybe because your already high-pitched voice just went up an octave, he thought, but refrained from stating aloud. "If there's something I should know, now's the time to speak up."

More silence.

"Sorry, Mr. Barrie. I'm needed in the cafeteria. I'm glad things are going well. Talk again soon." With a hasty good-bye, she hung up the phone.

Huh. He slowly set the handset back on the hook. What an odd phone call. Even for Susan.

He couldn't shake the feeling she'd neglected to mention something important.

CHAPTER 15

NATE

Nate shivered as he crossed the frost-covered ground, making his way toward the barn. Early morning sunlight crested the tree line, tinging the branches gold. Since sleep never came easy, he rose early, often before sunrise. This morning, he'd asked Frank if he could tour the roasting process, to which Frank grunted, "Be my guest," and went back to his cup of coffee and rumpled newspaper.

Apparently, some guy named Vick Johnson did most of the roasting these days. According to Beverly, if she hadn't insisted Frank slow down and hire help, he would've keeled over at the roaster years ago.

Nate hoped Vick wouldn't mind him watching a roast or two. Although he found the process intriguing, it would also serve as a distraction from a certain brunette he couldn't get out of his head. The anticipation of their outing to the middle school later that morning had his stomach twisted into knots. He hadn't been able to shake the feeling of her perfect hand clasped in his, or the way his skin smelled of her peppermint lotion long afterward.

When he entered the barn, he immediately noticed the shift in temperature. Warmth enveloped him, radiating from tall glass mason jars filled with piping-hot, freshly roasted coffee beans. And the smell—wow! Nate inhaled a deep breath, the earthy aroma so rich and heady, he could taste it.

A guy who looked a few years older than him stood near a large metal contraption. With his short haircut, rigid posture, and tattoo of an eagle on his muscular forearm, Nate pegged him as former military. Marine, maybe.

The guy flipped a switch, and the monstrous machine rumbled to life. After a second or two, smoke spilled from a chimney near the top, funneling through an opening in the roof. He turned, spotted Nate, then pulled out his earplugs as he strode toward him. "Hey. You must be Nate. Frank said you'd probably be stopping by sometime. I'm Vick."

"Nice to meet you." Nate shook his hand. "Mind if I stick around for a bit?"

"Not at all. I just started a roast, but once it's done, I'll walk you through the process."

"Cool. Thanks."

"Frank says you're a vet?"

"Army. You?"

"Marines."

They exchanged a nod of solidarity. While both branches of the military shared a healthy rivalry, Nate always viewed marines as his brothers in arms, albeit brothers in a big dysfunctional family. They gave each other a hard time, but also understood one another, since they frequently shared the same FOBs—forward operating bases—and were considered the military's "door kickers."

"How's it going?" Vick asked. He didn't need to clarify. Nate knew he meant *How are you adjusting to civilian life?*

"Like a walk in the park. Only the park is on fire."

"I know the feeling. It gets better."

"Yeah. I had a wake-up call about a year ago." *To put it mildly.* "I made some changes. Mind-over-matter type stuff. Focusing on the positive." He didn't really believe in manifesting his own destiny, but he never wanted to slip back into the hopeless abyss, which meant clinging to as much joy as possible—like Christmas.

Vick cocked his head thoughtfully. "Gratitude is good. You know what else helps?"

"Prozac?" Nate teased, then immediately regretted the quip. Prescription meds weren't anything to joke about. He would know.

Vick smiled. "Maybe. But I was going to say *people*. Community. The kind of family you forge one friendship at a time. Otherwise, what happens when the voices inside your head stop being so positive? I don't know about you, but my inner voice isn't always the most reliable. Or honest."

Nate understood the concept. He preached the same philosophy to other vets at the shelter. But while he was busy trying to be *their* support system, he'd neglected to build one of his own.

Before he could respond, a buzzer chimed. "Hold that thought," Vick said, trotting over to the roaster. "If I leave these beans in for a second too long, Frank'll notice. And if you think he's cranky now, wait'll you mess with his coffee." Flashing a rueful grin, Vick waved him over. "Come on, I'll show you how the magic happens."

For the next few hours, Vick walked Nate through several roasts, explaining the process in detail and even let him handle one on his own. While they worked, Nate almost wished he didn't have to head back to San Francisco at the end of the week.

If he were to ever build a support system, Vick would be the perfect guy to have on his team.

CHAPTER 16

JULIET

Juliet stared at the blinking cursor as snowflakes swirled past the window beyond her laptop screen, sparkling like flecks of glitter against the night sky. Cocooned in her very own wintry snow globe, surrounded by the pleasantly musty scent of old, leather-bound books, her fingers should be flying across the keyboard.

And yet, she couldn't conjure a single sentence, let alone ten chapters. So far, her quiet, distraction-free writing retreat hadn't turned out the way she'd planned.

That morning, she'd gone to the middle school with Nate, as promised. While she looked over the costumes with Eliza and her mother, Sylvia—the director of Poppy Creek's small theater company—Nate had worked on the sets with Luke and Eliza's husband, Grant, a local artist.

Every time she stole a glance at Nate above the clothing racks, she caught him looking at her. Once, he'd even smashed his own finger with the hammer, which made her feel terrible that he'd hurt himself, but also thrilled she'd been the subject of his attention.

She couldn't explain why, other than something had shifted between them during their outing to the tree farm yesterday. Nothing seismic or earth-shattering. Something subtle. But just enough to make her breath quicken whenever he walked into the room.

And tonight, knowing Frank and Aunt Beverly had decided to stay at their friend Dolores's until the storm passed, leaving her and Nate alone in the house, breathing normally commanded all her concentration.

The tempting aroma of something sweet and spicy wafting from the kitchen didn't help, either. She wouldn't have pegged Nate as a baker. But then, there were a lot of things she didn't know about him. A state of affairs she'd like to rectify.

She shut her laptop.

Don't do it, Jules. Stay in the study and get back to work.

She stood and smoothed out the crease in her wool skirt.

Put your backside back in that chair, young lady.

She tucked a strand of hair behind her ear. Her fingers twitched with nervous energy—nervous energy laced with excitement.

Ignoring the inner voice warning her to stay put, she followed the festive melody of "White Christmas" to the kitchen, pausing in the doorway.

Her racing heartbeat stuttered to a stop.

Nate stood at the butcher block island, the sleeves of his hunter-green Henley pushed up to his elbows. As he squeezed the handle of the antique flour sifter, his muscular forearm flexed.

Her faulty pulse revved to life, stumbling a few beats

before kicking into overdrive. She never knew a man could look so alluring coated in flour. Fried chicken, yes. That made sense. But a man? *Wow*. Her mouth watered.

He must have sensed her staring, because he lifted his gaze from the sifter. "Sorry, is the music too loud? I can turn it down." He reached for the phone in his front pocket.

"No, it's nice." It sounded like the original motion picture soundtrack of *White Christmas*, with all four stars of the film harmonizing together. The nostalgic notes conjured one of the few fond memories Juliet had with her mother during the holidays. She'd been nine, and her mother had put on the movie to distract her while she graded papers. Instead, her mother had been sucked into the film, too, and they'd watched it together with mugs of hot chocolate and buttered popcorn sprinkled with cinnamon and sugar.

Smiling at the memory, Juliet joined Nate at the small kitchen island. "What are you making?"

"It's supposed to be mince pie, but I can't seem to get it right." He frowned at a pie cooling on the stovetop. The blackened crust sank into the center.

"What recipe are you using?"

"The one in Cassie's book." He tipped his head toward the open Christmas Calendar on the counter. "Bake a mince pie is the day's task. Technically, I can check it off the list. But I'd like it to at least be edible, so I'm giving it another try."

"You're taking this Christmas Calendar seriously, aren't you?"

"Yes, ma'am." He looked so adorably earnest. Especially with a big smudge of flour on his right cheek.

She resisted the urge to wipe it away. With his hint of stubble, she expected his skin to be a little rough, but in a good way.

At the thought, her fingertips tingled. She curled them into her palm, dismissing the inappropriate impulse to touch a man she barely knew, no matter how attractive. *Get a grip, Jules.*

"I'll let you in on the secret to a perfect, flaky crust. It's a trick Aunt Beverly taught me."

"I'm all ears." He stepped to the side, making room for her at the island.

As she drew closer, she caught a heady whiff of pine and vetiver. Was it his soap? Cologne? Aftershave? It smelled heavenly. "First, we need a cheese grater."

"A cheese grater?" Nate grimaced. "You put cheese in your pie crust?"

"You don't have to look so horrified." She laughed. "It's for the butter."

While Nate found the cheese grater, she grabbed two sticks of butter from the overstuffed freezer.

"Now what?" He set the grater on the counter.

"Now, we turn all of this ice-cold buttercream into a big pile of fluffy snowflakes."

While she worked—gathering the golden shavings into a bowl—Nate watched over her shoulder, so close she could feel his body heat. For one brash second, she imagined his arms wrapping around her from behind. What if he took one more step and closed the gap between them?

Snap out of it, Jules. This isn't a Hallmark movie.

She concentrated on not scraping the skin off her fingers.

"Now we add it to the flour?" Nate asked when she'd finished. Was it her imagination or did his voice sound a little raspy, as if he had trouble breathing, too?

"Not yet. The friction from grating warmed up the butter. We have to cool it down again." She opened the freezer but couldn't find room for the bowl. Glancing out the window at the fluttering snowflakes, she had an idea. "Follow me."

They stepped into the stillness of the back porch, protected by the overhang, facing a tapestry of frosted pines. Before them, silvery moonlight illuminated a wonderland of white. As if on cue, the *White Christmas* soundtrack emanating from Nate's pocket emitted the timely song "Snow," the dulcet refrain serenading the idyllic scene.

She'd never witnessed anything more magical, and despite the chilly temperature, she stood in awed silence, basking in the unblemished beauty of the wintry woodland.

By her side, Nate murmured, "Whose woods these are I think I know. / His house is in the village though; / He will not see me stopping here / To watch his woods fill up with snow.'"

The poetic words of Robert Frost's "Stopping by Woods on a Snowy Evening" came to life before her eyes, so perfect and pure.

"'The woods are lovely, dark and deep, / But I have promises to keep,'" she whispered back, skipping ahead to her favorite stanza. "'And miles to go before I sleep.'"

"'And miles to go before I sleep,'" Nate repeated the last line, his voice low and reverent.

They stood side by side in companionable silence for a moment while "Count Your Blessings Instead of Sheep"—another song from the *White Christmas* soundtrack—played softly in the background. The poignant lyrics and soulful strain stirred something deep within her, drawing emotions she'd long suppressed.

"That poem always makes me sad," she admitted, shivering in the cold. The frigid air chilled all the way to her bones, but she didn't care. She didn't want the moment to end. "I get this sense that Frost wanted to stay longer, to admire nature's splendor. But he couldn't. Duty and obligation, whether external or self-imposed, stole his freedom to be present and enjoy one of God's gifts." She felt the same pressure—the pressure to constantly achieve, to prove her worth. How many simple pleasures had she missed in life, always striving for something greater?

"I don't want to be like the man in the poem," she confessed with a surge of conviction that sprang from deep within her soul. "We should make the most of every moment. And if there's something we've been wanting to do, we shouldn't put it off, right?"

She turned toward Nate, wondering if anything she'd said made any sense at all, wondering why she'd shared something so personal. He possessed this intangible quality —a quiet, steady presence—that made her feel safe to divulge her innermost thoughts, as if she instinctively knew she could trust him. Perhaps she could trust him with even more than her thoughts.

He gazed at her with a fire in his eye she'd never seen

before. With slow and deliberate movements, he took the bowl from her hands and set it on the railing. He took a step toward her, bridging the divide.

Gently, he cupped the side of her face, his palm warm against her skin.

She sucked in a breath, the cool air slipping past her slightly parted lips.

His gaze fell to her mouth, the firm pressure of his thumb tracing from her cheekbone to just beneath her chin.

He tilted her head, angling her lips toward his.

Her body trembled.

She arched her back, yearning to be closer, to be fully enveloped in his arms.

If he didn't kiss her soon, she'd melt into a puddle at his feet.

CHAPTER 17

NATE

Nate lost all sense of time and place, aware only of Juliet—of her presence, her scent, the feel of her skin.

From the moment they met, he couldn't deny her beauty or his attraction.

But now, her allure ran so much deeper than the physical. Her mind enthralled him. Not only her knowledge of poetry and literature, but her poignant insights. He wanted to know every thought she'd ever had, from the profoundly philosophical to the more mundane.

The desire to connect on a deeper level drove him to madness. How else could he explain his actions? He hadn't kissed anyone in years. Even when he dated, he didn't jump to the physical. He never kissed on a first date, let alone *before* a first date.

And yet, here he stood, staring into the most stunning eyes he'd ever seen, dark and velvety, like the richest French roast. But also soft and soulful, like a window into her innermost thoughts—the thoughts that captivated his undivided interest.

Her lips parted a centimeter more, as if granting him permission.

He lowered his head, his heart beating wildly.

This is it. The point of no return.

As his bottom lip grazed hers, covering his skin in goose bumps, the unexpected cadence of drums crashed through the stillness.

The military-style percussion emanating from his front pocket thrummed through his body, rewiring his brain.

His muscles tensed, and he bolted upright.

The peppy voices of Bing Crosby and Danny Kaye pounded in his ears as they merrily belted the jaunty lyrics to "Gee, I Wish I Was Back in the Army."

In a single instant, a switch flipped, leaving Nate disorientated, grappling to gain control of his emotions. Sweat slicked his palms, and he fumbled with his phone, shutting off the song before stuffing the cell back inside his pocket.

"Are you okay?" Juliet's concerned voice broke through the wall of confusion. She placed a hand on his chest. Could she feel his erratic heartbeat?

He couldn't find the words to answer her.

"Come with me." She led him by the hand into the sitting room, settling him on the couch in front of the fire. A moment later, she returned with a glass of water and sat beside him. "Do you want to talk about it?" she asked softly.

"I—" He hesitated, taking a gulp of water. It slid down his throat, crisp and cold. What could he say? He had no idea why he'd reacted so strangely to a harmless song.

There wasn't a simple explanation, no matter how badly he wanted one. "I'm fine."

She didn't respond at first, merely gazing into the flickering flames. After a minute or two of thoughtful silence, she asked, "Implicit flashback?"

He stared in surprise. "You know the term?"

"I've witnessed them quite a few times. I work for a nonprofit that aids women who've escaped domestic violence and human trafficking."

Nate studied her profile in the amber glow, stunned by what she'd shared. She continued to amaze him. And every new thing he learned about her made him like her even more. "I had no idea." Guess he shouldn't judge a book by its cover *or* bumper sticker.

She smiled. "We sort of skipped the get-to-know-you questions."

"I work part-time as a security guard at a jewelry store and volunteer at Forgotten Heroes." He suddenly wanted to lay everything on the table—to know every detail about her and to be fully known in return.

Her eyes widened. "You do? I thought—" She snapped her mouth shut.

"What?"

Her cheeks colored with the faint blush of embarrassment. "When my aunt said they'd agreed to host someone from the homeless shelter, I thought…" She trailed off as if she couldn't bring herself to finish the sentence.

Nate laughed a deep, rumbling laugh of disbelief.

"What's so funny?"

"Let me get this straight." He choked back another

chuckle. "You'd kiss a guy without a job or place to live, as long as he can pronounce Proust?"

She blinked, clearly not grasping the irony. "What are you talking about?"

"Your bumper sticker. 'If he can't pronounce Proust, then cut him loose.'"

"Oh!" Her hand flew to her mouth, stifling a giggle. "I'm borrowing my mom's car. That's her bumper sticker, not mine."

"That explains a lot." He'd learned a valuable lesson about jumping to conclusions.

"So, this whole time you had me down as—what? A literary snob?"

"Something like that."

"And yet, you still wanted to kiss me?" Her dark eyes danced with humor.

"*Wanted* to?" he repeated. "Past tense?" His lips twitched as he recalled the moment in Luke's truck when she'd said something similar.

"Well, I—uh—" she stammered, adorably flustered. Her pupils dilated, and his body responded to the physical cue, inching closer on the couch.

The delicate tendril grazing her cheek tempted him again, only this time, he gave in to the longing, stroking it lightly with his fingertips.

She shivered beneath his touch, her breath quickening.

He could so easily take her in his arms, blocking out the world—and every haunting memory from his past—with her perfect lips. But he didn't want to use her affection as a salve for his pain. Or take a single step further without removing any possible pretense. If he pursued Juliet, he wanted to do it right—with one hundred percent transparency.

Even if it ruined his chance with her.

"Jules," he said slowly, savoring the way the sweet syllable rolled off his tongue. "There's something I need to tell you."

"What is it?" she murmured in a sultry rasp that nearly sent him over the edge. As she spoke, she placed a hand on his forearm, stealing the words from his mouth with the simplest touch.

Once he told her the truth, would she still want him?

CHAPTER 18

NATE

Nate set his glass on the coffee table, his fingers shaking with nerves. The fire crackled in the hearth, offering him a comforting warmth as snow continued to fall beyond the bay window.

He felt Juliet's gaze as she sat in patient silence. *It's not fair to keep her waiting.* Gathering his courage in a fortifying breath, he turned to face her. "There's a reason I volunteer at the shelter. It saved my life once."

She didn't speak, but her eyes glinted with compassion, encouraging him to continue.

"Coming home from Iraq was harder than I thought. I—I couldn't sleep."

"Nightmares?" she asked gently.

"Sometimes. But mostly, I couldn't wind down enough to even fall asleep in the first place. I was in a constant state of high alert, no matter how hard I tried to relax." How could he explain the phenomenon of being so exhausted his bones ached and yet simultaneously wired with adrenaline?

"I'm so sorry, Nate. That sounds awful."

"I dealt with the insomnia for a while, but eventually, the lack of sleep made it difficult to function." He'd started forgetting things and making little mistakes that escalated into some pretty big ones, like leaving the stove on when he left the house. Dizziness and fatigue plagued him daily. Then came the headaches—manageable at first, then full-on skull-crushing migraines. Sometimes, he'd black out.

"When I struggled to hold down a job, I finally saw someone at the VA. They prescribed me sleeping pills." He hesitated as the memories came flooding back—memories that still hurt to relive.

"Did they help you sleep?"

"Yeah. A little too well." He closed his eyes, bracing against a surge of remorse. "The pills became an escape, day and night. When I took them, nothing existed anymore. Good, bad, past, present—it didn't matter. The world went completely blank. I felt"—he winced, ashamed to admit the truth—"free."

He opened his eyes, forcing himself to meet Juliet's gaze. He expected to see judgment. Revulsion. Pity. But he only saw tears. Tears of empathy and shared pain.

"I'm so sorry you went through that. I can't even imagine what it must have been like."

"I'm not proud of my choices. And I'm not trying to make excuses." He noticed he'd coiled his fist so tightly in his lap, his knuckles paled. But he couldn't stop now. She needed to know the whole truth. "It wasn't a conscious decision. More like a gradual numbing over time. I stopped going to work and paying my bills. Sometimes, I went days without eating. I'd given up."

He'd shared the story several times before with other vets he'd mentored, but sharing with Juliet felt different. Scarier. As if he had more to lose if her opinion of him changed.

"Just over a year ago, Susan, the director of Forgotten Heroes, found me passed out on a park bench. After she woke me up, she bought me coffee and a hot dog from a street vendor. Then she just sat with me, and we talked for hours. No one had done that before—asked for my story before making assumptions. I felt seen, actually *seen*, for the first time in years."

A tear slid down Juliet's cheek, and she didn't bother wiping it away. She displayed her tender, caring heart without hesitation. It was rare, and he'd never seen anything more beautiful.

"After Susan listened to my story, she gave me this." He pulled a small ceramic circle from his pocket. The jagged streak of gold down the center glimmered in the firelight.

"What is it? Is it—" Juliet peered closer at the hand-painted cherry blossoms. "A button?"

"Yeah, good guess." He cradled the precious token in his palm. "A vintage Japanese satsuma, more specifically. From the eighteenth century."

"It's gorgeous. The gold squiggle down the middle is an interesting design."

"It's called *kintsugi*. It's the Japanese art of repairing broken objects with gold. The custom has many meanings, but Susan says it reminds her that God not only makes broken things beautiful, He gives them a purpose. And part of that purpose is to share our story, our scars, so others know healing and restoration is possible. That's why I volunteer at the shelter. To tell others that they're never too broken. And they're never forgotten."

Juliet gently caressed the button, tracing the shimmering stripe of gold. When she finally spoke, her voice fluttered faintly, like a whispered thought still being formed. "The scars we bear are a badge, not a blemish. A testimony to the power of faith, hope—"

"And love," they said in unison.

Their eyes met, and her fingertip slid from the button to the palm of his hand. Her delicate touch trailed the sensitive contours of his skin, every callous and crease. His entire body tingled, hyperaware of each scintillating sensation.

Without thinking, he closed his hand over hers, lacing their fingers together. Their palms met, pressing the cool ceramic between them. With his free hand, he cupped her cheek, drawing her lips toward his. He paused with their mouths mere inches apart.

"If we do this," he murmured, his voice thick and raspy as he wrestled for restraint, "it means something. I can't walk away from this, from *you*. I can't kiss you and pretend it never happened. I'm all in, Jules. I'll do whatever it takes to be what you need, to make this work. I—"

"Nate," she whispered, her breath feather soft and sweet. "*Kiss me.*"

Eager to obey orders, he lowered his mouth to hers, gently at first, taking his time. But the more he lingered, savoring each second, the deeper his desire ran. With other women, there was always a discovery period, time to learn each other's rhythm. But with Juliet, the kiss came as naturally as breathing, fluid and passionate, like a poem that transcended the page.

It took all his self-control to reel himself back, but he wanted more than the physical with Juliet. He wanted all of her, to truly *know* her—the inner workings of her thoughts, beliefs, and secret longings. He craved the kind of connection carved in the quiet moments, from listening to every word, spoken and unspoken.

They spent the rest of the evening finishing the mince pie—which came out better when they made it together—sharing typical first-date anecdotes like favorite movies and hobbies, then delving into deeper territory like their childhood, faith, and their hopes and fears.

He shared things with Juliet he'd never told anyone before, not even Susan or his therapist at the VA. He even divulged the real reason he felt so drawn to Christmas, laying his entire heart on the table, open and bare. To his surprise and delight, she reciprocated with equal vulnerability. By the time he walked her to her room and kissed her good night, he knew with absolute certainty that he'd found a woman worthy of every poem ever written. A woman worth fighting for with every fiber of his being.

And from that moment on, nothing would ever be the same.

CHAPTER 19

JULIET

Juliet leaned against the door frame, her fingertips pressed against her lips. They still tingled from Nate's good-night kiss. In all her life, no man had ever kissed her like that. She tried to put the intensity of the experience into words, but not even *utterly transcendent* could do his kiss justice.

There was something special about Nate. He had this extraordinary way of looking at life, of turning a painful past into something positive—something powerful. He had an outlook—and a story—that should be shared.

At the thought, her gaze fell to her laptop occupying the small desk by the window, exactly where she'd left it earlier that evening. The smooth metallic case glowed in the golden light of the antique floor lamp.

Driven by an impulse she couldn't explain, she sat at the desk. The quiet whisper of wind swirled silver snowflakes past the frosted window, but she barely noticed, lost in a world of words inside her head as scenes and characters magically came into being.

She opened her laptop, and the screen blinked to life. Positioning her fingertips over the black backlit keys, she gathered a breath, then let the words flow freely, without judgment or overthinking.

Callie Holloway hated Christmas.

Candy canes made her cringe.

Santa Claus made her shudder.

And mistletoe... don't even get her started on mistletoe.

Didn't anyone see the irony in making a poisonous plant the official mascot of holiday romance? They might as well force couples to kiss under a sign that read, Your romantic dalliance is doomed to fail.

Juliet chuckled as the playful prose effortlessly appeared on the page. Why didn't anyone tell her writing could be so much fun?

Consumed with a creative energy she'd never experienced before, she indulged her secret, long-suppressed dream to write a "frivolous" romance novel. Without restraint or apology, she made a list of her favorite tropes —Opposites attract. Holiday homecoming. Unexpected inheritance—jotting down notes on how they'd each unfold. With every punctuated *click* of the keys, her heart beat faster, bursting with artistic anticipation.

By the time she paused to take a break, the characters felt like close friends. For the heroine, Callie Holloway, she borrowed bits and pieces from women she'd met at Reclaim, mixing in a pinch of herself. As a result, Callie felt real, with a personality—and challenges to overcome—that rang true to life. Her hero, Private Nick Anderson, bore a more direct resemblance to her inspiration, mirroring Nate's backstory almost word for word.

Exhausted and exhilarated, she leaned back in the chair, stretching her fingers. She gazed in awe at the wealth of words sprawled across the screen, shocked by how much she'd accomplished in a relatively short amount of time.

In a few hours, she'd completed a comprehensive outline and five solid chapters. But what would she do with them? She loved what she'd created, but a romance novel wouldn't live up to her parents' expectations *or* her editor's. Besides, she'd stolen Nate's life story. His private, intimate thoughts and experiences weren't hers to tell. She wouldn't do anything to exploit him or betray his trust.

And yet, she couldn't bear to delete all her hard work, either.

She saved the document onto her desktop under the acronym SCP for *A Soldier's Christmas Promise*, surprised by the physical ache she felt knowing the unfinished story would never see the light of day. These characters didn't even exist a few hours ago, so why did it hurt so much to say goodbye?

Before she could give the question more serious thought, her phone buzzed, signaling an incoming text.

Hi, sweetheart. Just got a call from Debra.

Uh-oh. Why was her editor calling her mother? Whatever the reason, it probably wasn't good news.

Buzz. Another text.

She's going to Singapore for New Year's and won't have a chance to read your chapters until she gets back.

Juliet felt her pulse skip a few beats, daring to hope. Would this mean an extension on her deadline? *Please say she's giving me more time.* Holding her breath, Juliet stared at the three dots indicating her mother was composing another text.

I know you're excited and want to keep the ball rolling, so rather than postpone, I told her you'd email your chapters early, by the end of this week.

Juliet stared at the screen, reading the text again. No, no, no... This couldn't be happening. Please, no. Tears burned at the backs of her eyes as guilt and panic swelled in her chest.

She'd wasted so much time succumbing to her writer's block, hanging her entire career on the ridiculous hope that some spectacular storyline would miraculously appear in her mind. She should've tried harder; she should've forced a story onto the page. Instead, she'd lived in denial at the expense of her future—of her parents' respect.

And what did she have to show for her months of fear-induced avoidance? Absolutely nothing.

As she read the next text from her mother, a tear slid down her cheek, scorching her skin with shame.

Let me know if I overstepped, sweetheart. But I told Debra, I know my daughter. She's a Klein, through and through. Ink runs in our blood. I said, Juliet probably has twenty chapters by now. And I know every one of them is brilliant. XXO

Sick to her stomach, Juliet dropped her head in her hands, surrendering to her tears. She had four days to turn in ten chapters with aplomb. Ten *extraordinary* chapters worthy of awards. Or implode her career before it ever got started. A career that she'd only just realized she wanted for herself, not merely to please her parents.

That night, somewhere amid the joyful haze of creative inspiration, she'd discovered a startling truth.

Her literary aspiration ran deeper than living up to a lofty family legacy.

She had an authorial dream all her own.

It just wasn't a dream that would make her parents proud.

CHAPTER 20

FRANK

F rank stood at the kitchen window and sipped his morning coffee, watching Nate and Juliet build a snowman in the backyard—Day 5 on the Christmas Calendar. Something had happened last night while he and Bevy stayed over at Dolores's, waiting out the storm. Even from afar, he could see the change in their interactions, the playful way they threw snowballs at each other, their easy laughter.

As soon as they got home that morning and Bevy noticed two mugs and dessert plates drying on the dish rack, she'd predicted the shift in their relationship. "Mark my words," she'd said with a satisfied smile, "those two finally had a real conversation last night and realized they're perfect for each other."

Based on the lovey-dovey display he was witnessing—Nate pulled Juliet into his arms before diving into a powdery snowdrift while she squealed in feigned protest—Bevy was right. Too bad she had to rush off to the library and couldn't bask in the success of her matchmaking scheme. Maybe they should invite Nate to stay with them a little longer so he and Juliet could spend Christmas together?

Frank harrumphed into his coffee cup. He really had gone soft in his old age. When had he ever wanted to extend the visit of a houseguest? Muttering about Bevy's bad influence, he served himself some mince pie.

He'd moved on to a second slice by the time Nate and Juliet stumbled through the back door, pink-cheeked and breathless.

"Good morning." Nate tugged off his knit cap. His blue eyes shone clear and bright, the look of a man unabashedly smitten. "That coffee smells great."

"Help yourself." Frank nodded toward the French press on the counter.

"Thanks, but I gotta get going. I'm meeting Luke at the middle school to work on the sets." His gaze flickered to Juliet, as if he dreaded the thought of leaving her. *Ah, young love.*

"If you see Cassie," Juliet said, hanging her coat on a hook by the door, "please tell her I'm almost finished with the script. I should have it done by tomorrow. Or the day after, at the absolute latest."

"I'll let her know." The two lovebirds stood staring at each other for several seconds until Frank cleared his throat.

Nate snapped to attention. "Well, I'm off. See you guys later."

"Bye." Juliet blushed as Nate shot her a lingering glance before slipping out of the kitchen.

Good grief. The romantic chemistry between those two

hung so thick in the air he could almost chew it, and he vastly preferred the taste of pie. He took another bite and washed it down with a gulp of French roast.

Juliet poured herself a cup and joined him at the kitchen table, plopping onto her chair with a blissful sigh. She wore the same besotted expression as Nate.

Frank remembered the early days of falling in love, when eating and sleeping gave way to thoughts of Bevy and Bevy alone. The constant daydreams of the future, both thrilled and terrified by the endless possibilities, the uncertainty of it all. If he'd met Bevy during the time he wrote his first book, he doubted *The Mariposa Method* would've made it into existence.

"How's the novel coming along?" he asked Juliet, taking advantage of their first moment alone.

"Smooth sailing." The light in her eyes dimmed, and her features strained, revealing her lie.

"I milked a giraffe this morning," he said casually, taking another sip.

"S-sorry?"

"I thought we were both sharing things that aren't true."

"Oh." Her shoulders slumped. "Is it that obvious?"

"You have a tell."

"What is it?"

"Your face."

Juliet sputtered with laughter, caught off guard by his remark. Some of her tension slipped away. "Okay. You're right. It hasn't been going well. *At all.*"

"Writer's block?"

"I guess." With both hands wound around the mug, she stared intently into the velvety liquid, studying the tendrils of aromatic steam. "To be honest, ever since I got here, I've had plenty of inspiration, just not the right kind of inspiration."

He nodded, encouraging her to elaborate.

Instead, she asked, "When you wrote *The Mariposa Method*, how did you know that was the book you were meant to write?"

"It was the story only I could tell."

"And it revolutionized the coffee industry, hitting all the bestseller lists."

"I didn't set out to revolutionize anything. Or make any list."

"So, your success came without even trying?" The possibility seemed to depress her even more.

"Oh, I tried. I'd never worked harder on anything in my life. But I had my own goalposts."

"What were they?"

"For starters, to end the world's biggest crisis: bad coffee." He flashed a wry grin.

She smiled and toasted him with her mug. "And the world thanks you."

Taking a more serious tone, he asked, "You want to know the truth?"

"Very much."

"I'd found something I was passionate about and couldn't keep it to myself. Like a compulsion. I needed people to see their daily dose of caffeine differently. To see what I did. Because it made my life a bit better, and I wanted it to do the same for them."

"That sounds pretty revolutionary," she murmured.

"You know what's revolutionary? Writing what's in here." He tapped his chest above his heart. "You can study the market and write what you think will sell to the masses or appease the critics. There's nothing wrong with that. But you can't control other people, which means you can't guarantee that kind of success, even if you give it your best shot. Besides," he added, softening his tone with a note of compassion. "I don't think that's what you really want. Otherwise, you wouldn't be having so much trouble getting your horse out of the starting gate."

She met his gaze, and he could see her internal struggle reflected in her dark, expressive eyes.

"I won't lie and say writing the story of your heart will secure you a spot on the bestsellers list," he told her. "But it can guarantee you success, as long as you redefine your definition and make it your own."

She dropped her gaze, peering into her mug thoughtfully. The aromatic tendrils of steam had long dissipated, which meant her coffee would be lukewarm soon. Normally, he wouldn't abide such an atrocity.

But today, he'd let it slide.

Some things—like the personal breakthrough of an aspiring author—were more important than coffee. Although, he'd never admit that aloud.

CHAPTER 21

NATE

Nate sat at a table by the window while Luke chatted with his wife as she worked her magic on the espresso machine. Cassie had offered them free coffee and cinnamon rolls as a thank-you for all their hard work revamping the pageant set pieces.

Passersby strolled along Main Street, bundled in thick coats and warm mittens, but Nate barely noticed them. He hadn't touched his fresh-from-the-oven cinnamon roll, either, despite its mouthwatering aroma. His distracted mind swirled with scattered thoughts.

In a matter of days, he'd not only fallen hard for Juliet, but for the town of Poppy Creek, too. He appreciated the slower pace, friendly people, and strong sense of camaraderie that permeated the close-knit community. More than once, he'd wondered what it would be like to stay here permanently.

"Cass made you a special latte." Luke set a tall glass mug on the table and sat across from him. "But if you don't like it, she's happy to make you something else."

"I'm sure it's great." Nate took a sip. The sweetness of creamy eggnog blended into spicy notes of nutmeg and cinnamon with a hint of clove. It tasted like Christmas in a cup. "Okay, I think this is the best latte I've ever tasted." How had she known exactly what he wanted when he didn't even know himself?

"She has an innate talent for this stuff." Luke glanced over his shoulder, tossing his wife an adoring smile. The same smile Nate suspected he'd been wearing all morning with Juliet. "Speaking of talent," he added. "You have a real knack for woodworking. Do you have previous experience?"

"Nothing formal. Just a few skills I've picked up along the way." He hesitated, wondering if he should elaborate. He didn't usually share details from his past, except for during discussions with mentees, when he thought the anecdotes might help them. But something about Luke put him at ease, as if he'd known him for decades. "For most of my teen years, I lived in a group home. There was this staff member—Rodrigo—who set up a small shop class in the backyard on the weekends. I guess he thought teaching us a useful life skill would put us on the right path."

"Did it work?"

"For a few guys, yeah. It gave us a sense of purpose, made us feel like we could actually be good at something after a lifetime of feeling worthless. It also helped that you had to earn the privilege by following the house rules. They weren't going to hand the hardcore troublemakers a wood-carving kit."

"Smart." Luke sipped his coffee, peering at him thoughtfully. "Rodrigo sounds like a good guy. And he gave you a solid foundation. Plus, you have a lot of natural talent. And you follow directions well."

"Thank the army for that." Nate saluted, and Luke smiled.

"I'll cut to the chase." Luke set his mug on the table. "I'd like to hire you. I've been needing an extra set of hands for a while, but never found the right person. I think you're that person. For the first few months, you'd learn the ropes, working on custom furniture pieces with my supervision, as well as taking on the role of delivery driver once they're done. When you're ready, you can work on your own projects. It would be a full-time position with a competitive hourly wage, and plenty of room to grow. What do you think?"

Nate struggled to process Luke's proposition. Luke wanted to hire him? To make custom furniture? Surely he'd misheard. Or maybe hallucinated?

"If you're worried about living arrangements, there's an apartment above the antiques store on Main Street that needs a new tenant. And I could negotiate a good rent, since the owner is my sister-in-law." Luke grinned again.

The guy was actually serious. He'd officially offered him his dream job. "Wow, man. I—I don't know what to say."

"How about, you'll take the job?"

"Can I think about it?" Part of him wanted to jump at the chance. A very *large* part. Until someone offered to pay him to read books for a living, he couldn't handpick a more ideal situation. But what about Dozer and the other vets at the shelter? And what about Juliet? She'd be heading back to San Francisco after the holidays. Presently, they lived in the same city. Why mess that up?

"Of course. Take your time. I got a little carried away in my excitement and dumped the idea on you out of the blue. But I think we work well together, and this could be a great opportunity for both of us. I didn't want to pass up the possibility."

Luke was right. They did work well together. And he couldn't ask for a better boss. From a career standpoint, he'd be a fool to turn down Luke's offer.

But on a personal level, he had a lot to lose. Maybe *too* much.

CHAPTER 22

JULIET

Drawing near the end of a two-day writing binge, Juliet gazed at her laptop screen, her tired, bleary eyes straining to read the final words of her novel, *A Soldier's Christmas Promise*.

After her conversation with Frank yesterday, she'd given herself permission to write from the heart without confining herself to other people's expectations. As a result, the words had poured out of her like a creative wellspring formerly untapped. She'd never known writing could be so collaborative, as if she'd written in tandem with her characters. But once she knew and understood them—their wounds, hopes, and fears—they'd steered the story, from Chapter One to The End.

Still in disbelief that she'd written an entire novel in a matter of days—albeit an extremely rough draft of one— she read back over her final words, blinking against a sudden surge of tears.

As Nick stared at the towering pine, draped in ribbons and sparkling lights, a startling truth solidified in his heart.

Christmas wasn't a coping mechanism. Or a to-do list. It was a celebration. A celebration of the life-changing love bestowed in a lowly manger—God's gift of hope to the world.

He'd come to the small town of Thistle River in search of a light bright enough to dim the darkness inside him. He thought he'd find it among the festive trappings and trimmings, but he'd looked in all the wrong places. In the end, Nick found God's love reflected in the kindness of others, like the brightest star in the sky guiding him to where he belonged—to the family of his heart.

He reached for Callie's hand, entwining their fingers. She leaned her head against his shoulder, so instant and innate, as if she'd done it all her life.

"Almost ready to go home?" she asked, snuggling against him in the chilly night air.

He nestled his cheek against her hair, savoring the sweet scent of the silky-soft strands. "I'm already there," he whispered. "I'm already there."

Juliet sat perfectly still, immobilized by an unfamiliar emotion. Was it satisfaction in her own work? Self-respect? Although she knew the manuscript would require some serious editing, she loved the world and characters she'd created. Dare she admit, she felt almost proud?

But as soon as the euphoric feeling settled in her heart, another more powerful emotion took over—*fear.* Fear of what her editor would say when she submitted a romance novel, not the literary masterpiece she'd promised. And worse—what would her parents say? Would they be embarrassed? Ashamed? Disappointed? What if they didn't want anything to do with her and her silly, derivative book?

The agonizing, unanswered questions assaulted her at

an alarming speed, almost stealing every ounce of joy she'd earned by finally writing The End. Luckily, she had two more days before her new deadline. She'd planned to use the time to rewrite Nick's character and make him less identical to Nate, even though the prospect made her sadder than it should. Nick was a fictional character, after all, so she knew it was the right thing to do.

Plus, the two extra days would help her gather her courage. And hopefully, she'd devise the perfect way to tell her parents. At the mere thought of the impending conversation, anxiety fluttered erratically in her chest like a frantic bird with a wounded wing. She tried to push the topic from her mind. She deserved a break, and that night, she'd get to share her favorite Poppy Creek tradition with Nate—Pajama Christmas. The quirky tree-lighting ceremony—where everyone in town wore festive PJs—had even inspired the final scene of her novel. And now, she'd get to live out the romantic moment herself.

Don't let fear of the future steal your present joy, she reminded herself.

She mentally repeated the mantra as she walked into the living room moments later, clad in the plaid flannel pajamas Aunt Beverly had picked out. When she reached the threshold, she paused, rendered speechless by the sight before her. Nate stood by the fireplace, wearing a matching pair of PJs. With one arm propped against the mantel, he leaned forward, gazing into the flickering flames. The golden glow highlighted his chiseled features. With his strong, muscular frame filling out the festive ensemble, he looked both ruggedly handsome and adorably snuggable.

He must have sensed her presence because he straightened and met her gaze. In an instant, a glimpse of their future flashed before her eyes. It was Christmas morning, and they were cuddled on the couch in front of the fire while their posse of children—both biological and foster—tore open their presents. The image was so visceral and intense, her throat went dry.

Get a grip, Jules. It's fiction. And way too soon for thoughts like that.

She blamed her recent writing sessions for putting romance on the brain.

Don't overthink it. Just enjoy a sweet, sexy man decked out in the softest fabric ever invented. You don't need to skip to happily ever after just yet.

She tried to focus on breathing normally while begging her cheeks not to turn bright pink. But the way Nate looked at her—like a starving man presented with an extravagant Christmas feast—wasn't helping.

"Well, don't you two look cute as a button," Aunt Beverly cooed, coming in from the kitchen. She wore the same plaid flannel, only sewn into a long nightgown with lace ruffles at the cuffs and collar.

Frank trudged behind her wearing a matching nightshirt and floppy Scrooge-style nightcap. "We look ridiculous."

"We're festive, darling. It's part of the fun."

"Is freezing to death the other part?"

"You may wear your coat over your pajamas," she said patiently. "Just don't button it up all the way."

Juliet shared an amused smile with Nate as he helped her into her coat. Frank tried to be a good sport most of the time, but the man had his limits. Apparently, wearing a long flannel nightshirt in public crossed the line. Luckily, by the time they arrived at the town square and joined the flurry of festivities, his spirits had lifted.

Between the live band performing holiday favorites, the magical glow of twinkle lights glittering across the square, and a plethora of booths offering mouthwatering treats like chocolate-covered sugar plums, deep-fried fruitcake, and sticky toffee pudding on a stick, it was impossible to be anything but merry and bright.

Nibbling on a shared bag of peanut brittle popcorn, Juliet and Nate stood side by side, staring at the small stage in eager anticipation of the official tree-lighting ceremony. Every time their elbows bumped or their fingers grazed, a shiver of delight skittered up her arm. Would this heavenly feeling ever fade? She hoped not.

"That's an impressive tree." Nate gazed at the towering pine draped in hundreds of bulbs, waiting to be lit.

"Each ornament was handmade by schoolchildren." She fondly recalled being able to participate when she was younger.

"That reminds me." Nate cleared his throat, and the energy between them suddenly shifted. Why did he look so nervous? "I made you something." He reached into his coat pocket and retrieved a small object wrapped in gold paper.

"When did you have time to make me something?"

"It's no big deal."

She handed him the bag of popcorn so she could unwrap his gift. Her pulse thrummed as she carefully peeled back the paper. Nestled inside the wrapping sat a wooden ornament shaped like a book. In the center, Nate had carved the outline of a heart.

Tears welled in her eyes.

"It's an ornament to commemorate this year, like your aunt's tradition." Nate shuffled his feet. "I know you're nervous about your debut living up to everyone's expectations, but I don't think you should worry. You have the biggest heart, and as long as you pour even an ounce of it into your book, I'm confident the story will be exactly what it needs to be."

His sweet words of encouragement spoke to her lingering fears and doubts, echoing Frank's advice. She'd come to Poppy Creek looking for isolation, but it was community—people to speak truth into her life—that she'd needed all along.

She thought of the manuscript sitting on her laptop back at the house. If only Nate knew how instrumental he'd been in helping her overcome her writer's block. One day, when the story was ready, she'd tell him.

She lifted the ornament by its silky red ribbon, finally finding her voice. "Thank you, Nate. It's the most beautiful ornament I've ever seen." Peering closer, she admired the intricate details—the way he'd carved grooves for each of the pages and decorated the spine. "You have a real gift for this. You could sell these."

"Funny you should say that." He dug his fingers through his hair. "Luke offered me a job yesterday."

The world shifted in and out of focus as Juliet tried to wrap her brain around the news. Nate might stay in Poppy Creek? What would that mean for their relationship? "Wow. That—that's amazing. Did you accept his offer?" She tried to keep her tone steady.

"I told him I need to think about it. It's tempting. Job-wise, it's everything I could want. But there are downsides."

"There are?" She forced herself to meet his gaze, holding her breath.

"There are a dozen reasons to stay in San Francisco. One in particular." The meaning behind his words, and the depth of his gaze, made her stomach spin.

He would turn down the job to be with her? For a moment, she wanted to shout for joy. But her elation quickly gave way to uncertainty. How would she feel if he gave up a dream for her? "You should take it," she blurted before her brain could catch up with her heart.

"What?"

"You should take the job," she repeated, surprising herself.

"You really think so?" He frowned, looking almost as if she'd hurt his feelings.

She hastened to explain. "Obviously, I don't love the idea of being apart. But Luke's offer is an amazing opportunity. And it's perfect for you." She gathered a breath, fighting the selfish urge to change her mind. "I know the shelter is important to you, but you can still find a way to help out. And as far as we're concerned—" Was she really saying this? "We can make it work. San Francisco is only a few hours away."

He titled his head, seriously contemplating her suggestion. "Are you sure?"

"Positive," she lied, plastering on a smile.

"Okay," he said slowly, "then I guess I'll consider it."

"Great." Still smiling like a maniac, she turned her gaze

toward the makeshift stage. *Whatever you do, don't cry. It will all work out just fine.*

She barely heard a word of Cassie's speech or noticed the way the illuminated tree transformed the town square into a kaleidoscope of colors, mirroring the idyllic scene she'd written earlier that evening.

Her mind reeled with worst-case scenarios.

She'd meant what she said about Nate pursuing his dream job.

But what if happily ever after existed only in romance novels and didn't extend to real life?

CHAPTER 23

JULIET

Juliet dug her hands into the chilled cookie dough, still reeling from last night's conversation with Nate. Would he really accept Luke's job offer and stay in Poppy Creek? She'd tried to put the possibility out of her mind all morning to focus on editing her manuscript. She'd even brainstormed dozens of different backstories for Nick, but each time she tried to make changes to his character, the whole story felt off somehow.

Distracted and frustrated, she'd abandoned her laptop in favor of butter, eggs, and flour. She'd read somewhere that basic manual tasks could help reset the brain. Maybe baking sugar cookies would be the cure she needed?

With a satisfying *thwack*, she slapped the rolling pin against the ball of dough, pressing with a little more force than necessary. *Ah.* The motion offered more stress relief than she'd expected. She continued to drag the rolling pin back and forth, letting her mind wander.

What if I wrote Nick as a Christmas tree farmer with debilitating pollen allergies? Or an artisan baker who suddenly develops a gluten intolerance? Or a dog groomer who can't handle pet dander?

Juliet groaned at her feeble attempts to change Nick's backstory and still maintain a compelling character. Besides, *A Dog Groomer's Christmas Promise* didn't have quite the same ring to it.

The clatter of the rolling pin against the counter drew her attention to the task at hand. She'd rolled the dough so thin she could see the wood grain of the butcher block. *Great. Time to start over.*

She scraped the dough back into a ball with her bare hands, relishing the tactile sensation of the soft, spongy texture. For fun, she formed the dough into three circular mounds, stacking them like a snowman.

"Cute. Not sure how evenly it'll bake, though." Nate stood in the doorway, gazing at her with the most adorable grin.

At the mere sight of him, all the stress drained from her body, replaced by an intense longing to be held by him, to bask in his comforting presence.

As if on cue, he bridged the divide and pulled her into his arms. She melted into him, inhaling his soothing scent while simultaneously blinking back tears. They'd only just found each other. If he stayed in Poppy Creek, how would she survive being separated?

"I've missed you," he said softly into her hair.

The last few days, he'd been beyond supportive, giving her ample time and space to write without a single complaint.

Swallowing the lump in her throat, she murmured, "Missed you, too." And if he moved to Poppy Creek, she'd go on missing him. "How are the sets coming along?" she asked, avoiding the one question she really wanted to ask. *And what about the job?* He'd tell her when he was ready.

"Great. All finished! In fact, Luke said to tell you he plans to swing by soon to grab a copy of the play, so Cassie can make copies for the kids."

"Oh, right! Of course." She'd texted Cassie that morning to tell her she'd finished. She glanced at her sticky hands. "I'll just quickly wash up."

"Want me to grab it for you?"

"You don't mind?"

"Nope. And I accept cookies as a form of payment."

"Deal." She grinned. "My laptop is wirelessly connected to Frank's printer, so all you have to do is pull up the file and hit Print."

"I think I can handle that."

"A man of many talents," she teased. "The file is labeled *School Christmas Pageant*. It's on my desktop."

"Got it." He pressed a quick kiss to her forehead before striding out of the kitchen.

"The login password for the laptop is *charles dickens*. Two words, all lowercase," she called after him, blissfully aware that she trusted him completely.

CHAPTER 24

NATE

Nate smiled as he typed the password into Juliet's laptop and watched the screen flicker to life, thrilled by their mutual trust. They may not have known each other for very long, but there was a depth to their relationship that took some couples years to cultivate.

His smile deepened into a bemused, affectionate grin when he caught sight of her cluttered, chaotic desktop. She must have a hundred files and folders scattered across the screen without any discernible system. But what some people might find exasperating, he viewed as merely another one of her endearing quirks.

Although, after a few minutes of unsuccessful searching for the *School Christmas Pageant* file, he wouldn't mind if her laptop was a bit more organized. Finally, he spotted a file titled *SCP*. School Christmas Pageant? The acronym matched. That had to be the right one. He double-clicked, and the document filled the screen.

His gaze immediately registered the name Nick Anderson. Oddly close to Nate Henderson. His brain warned him to stop reading. He'd clearly opened the wrong file—this was a novel, not a play—but familiar words jumped off the page, keeping his attention rooted in place.

On the outside, Nick Anderson loved Christmas. He was a regular Clark Griswold in combat boots. Only, deep down, it wasn't the bright lights and big, elaborate parties that drew him to the festive holiday. He longed for what Christmas represented —the season for family. The kind of family Nick didn't have.

Those were *his* words. Confidential thoughts and feelings he'd shared with Juliet the night of the snowstorm, that he'd never told anyone else.

He scrolled through the document, scanning various lines and phrases, trying to wrap his head around what he was reading.

She'd turned him into a character in her novel. A romance novel, as far as he could tell. Private Nick Anderson looked, sounded, and even had thoughts just like him. Had she shown this to anyone yet? Submitted it to her editor, even?

He suddenly felt exposed and vulnerable, as if his personal wounds had been paraded around the literary world without his permission. His heart racing, he skipped to the last few pages, consumed by a morbid curiosity.

So far, Juliet had copied his life story nearly word for word. But how would she end it?

As Nick stared at the towering pine, draped in ribbons and sparkling lights, a startling truth solidified in his soul. Christmas wasn't a coping mechanism. Or a to-do list. It was a celebration. A celebration of the life-changing love bestowed in a lowly manger—God's gift of hope to the world.

A sudden warmth swept across Nate's chest, spreading

to his fingertips. Compelled by the resonance of her words, he kept reading.

In the end, Nick found God's love reflected in the kindness of others, like the brightest star in the sky guiding him to where he belonged—to the family of his heart.

Nate swallowed, surprised by the lump of emotion constricting his throat. Moments ago, he'd felt exploited, maybe even a little betrayed. But now?

"Hey, what's taking so long in—" Juliet's cheerful tone faltered the minute she walked into the room and caught him standing over her laptop, the novel open on the screen. "N-Nate?" Her voice warbled with uncertainty.

He slowly turned, his thoughts whirling, struggling to fall into place. His conflicted emotions must have played out across his face, because Juliet's eyes widened woefully.

She stood a few feet away from him, her features ashen. "It—it's not what you think." She wrung her hands, twisting her fingers together like tangled tinsel. "I'd planned to rewrite Nick's character before I sent the story to my editor. I would never, *ever* betray your privacy. Please believe me."

Her dark eyes glinted like a window to her soul, and inside, he could see her heart breaking.

"Please, say something," she begged, hoarse and tearful. "I know this looks bad. But I promise, I'm going to rewrite every single word of Nick's backstory before I send the novel to my editor. When I'm done, it won't bear even the faintest resemblance to your life story."

As her words sank in, he believed them. And he knew he should accept her explanation and leave it at that. They could move on and never speak of the incident again.

But he couldn't let it go. Not after what he'd read.

CHAPTER 25

JULIET

Juliet trembled, waiting for Nate to respond. Dread mixed with desperation, leaving her dizzy. She couldn't lose him over this—a foolish, fixable mistake. *Please, please say something.*

"That's a shame," he said slowly.

Juliet blanched, completely taken aback. *What did he say?* She'd expected him to be upset, hurt, maybe even angry, at what she'd done. Even though she hadn't planned to publish her novel as is, she knew how it looked, how it might make him feel. He had every right to air his grievances. So, why were his features soft, so affectionate?

Adding to her shock, a slow smile spread across his face. "I admit, I was upset when I first saw what you'd written. But then, I realized that would make me a hypocrite. I'd just given you a whole speech about how our scars are meant to be shared."

"But by us, on our own terms," she corrected, still reeling from his unexpected response. "I had no right to use your story for my own. It's yours to tell, not mine."

"Maybe," he said thoughtfully. Glancing back at her laptop, he ran his fingers through his hair, as if searching for what to say. "But maybe not." He met her gaze again, his eyes warm with admiration. "What you've written is really good, Jules. Great, even. You've told my story in a way I never could. And honestly, made it a whole lot more accessible to way more people. You have a way with words. A gift."

At his words and expression of loving, unbridled pride, a wave of emotion crashed into her, cleansing and bolstering all at once. She wanted to write them down, to imprint them on her heart with an everlasting ink. No man —no *person*—had ever made her feel this way before. As if she had something worthy to contribute to the world.

"What you're doing is important, Jules. And I don't want a little bit of discomfort on my part to get in the way of that."

"Important?" she echoed, caught off guard by his word choice. Her novel may be good but hardly *important* in the grand scheme of things. At least, not to anyone but her. "It's just a romance novel," she said, in case he hadn't read enough to discern the genre.

"There's no such thing as *just* a romance novel. All books are special. They can evoke any number of emotions, from anger to outrage, grief and empathy, even joy. Especially joy." His eyes clouded for a moment, turning a deep, hazy blue. "There's so much sadness in the world, Jules. I've seen it. I've been mired in its darkness. And if you can make the world even a little bit brighter with your books, that's as worthy a goal as any award or recognition. If you want to tell my story—or use any part of it—it's yours. I trust you with my life, even in print."

As Nate spoke, tears of wonder and overwhelming gratitude trailed down her cheeks. How had she ever existed without this man? His view of the world—and her place in it—was so much richer and fuller than she'd ever imagined.

She crossed the room, and their lips met in a kiss that spoke all the words in her heart—words that transcended time and logic.

She loved this man for his strength of character and his kindness.

And no amount of distance between them would take that away.

CHAPTER 26

NATE

Nate quietly closed the study door, leaving a piece of his heart behind with Juliet—a woman unlike anyone he'd ever met.

Once he'd recovered from the shock of seeing his innermost thoughts in print, he'd experienced a rush of awe and admiration. For as long as he could remember, he'd loved the written word. Books had been his lifeline in the hard times, his friends and mentors—*his family*.

And now he'd fallen for a woman who could weave words into a brand-new world, like every author who'd invited him into their heart and soul, creating a safe space when he'd needed an escape. Now, he got to be a part of the process, both as a reader and a muse.

As he pictured Juliet, perched at the tiny desk in the study, polishing her manuscript before sending it off to her editor, he stopped halfway down the hall, stunned by the sudden depth of emotion. How was it possible to feel this deeply for someone he'd just met?

He wanted to spend the rest of his life with this woman,

discovering new details about her every day, learning to love her better. Was it too soon for thoughts like this? *Probably.* But he doubted he'd have much luck scrubbing them from his brain.

Giving her the space she needed to write, he took the back steps two at a time, heading for the roastery.

Vick stood alone at the long wooden table, scooping hot, crackling coffee beans into a tall five-gallon mason jar. He nodded in welcome when he spotted Nate enter the barn.

"Mind if I hang out for a while?" Nate asked.

"As long as you don't mind if I put you to work." Vick grinned.

"What can I do?"

"Hand me that other jar."

Nate set the empty mason jar on the table, then moved the jar Vick had just filled with beans out of the way. Heat radiated off the glass, warming his cold hands.

"How long have you been roasting for Frank?"

"A few years."

"I would've guessed a lot longer than that." Vick worked as if the movements were second nature.

"Frank's a great teacher. Any interest in learning to roast?"

"Me? No. But my friend Dozer would love it. He raves about the coffee at the shelter. He'd flip if he got to meet the guy who roasts it."

"So invite him. I'll put him to work, too." Vick smiled, but Nate couldn't tell if he was being serious.

"Invite him? Just like that?"

"Sure. Why not?"

"Because it's not my house."

"He can bunk with me for a day or two if he doesn't mind crashing on the couch. Or a mischievous miniature goat nibbling on his shoes." Vick chuckled.

"Seriously? You'd invite a stranger into your home without a second thought?" The people of Poppy Creek were unreal.

"He's a vet?"

"Marine."

"Then he's not a stranger, is he?"

Vick's words struck a chord that resonated with Nate on a soul level. A shared experience like military service—especially combat—tied you to someone in an intense, inexplicable way with a bond thicker than blood.

Nate mulled over Vick's suggestion. Could he invite Dozer? The more he thought about his friend meeting Vick, Frank, Beverly, Luke, and especially Juliet, the more he liked the idea. Poppy Creek had changed his life. Maybe it would do the same for Dozer? Heaven knows, he needed it.

"I suppose I could take the rest of the day to go pick him up." Juliet would be writing, anyway.

"There's also a bus route that runs from San Francisco into Primrose Valley, one town over. You could pick him up there," Vick offered.

"Good to know. Thanks." Nate's heart thrummed as the spontaneous plan took shape. This might actually work. He'd be leaving in two days, anyway, so Dozer could catch a ride back with him.

At the thought, his heartbeat stalled, revealing the truth he wasn't ready to admit. He didn't want to leave Poppy

Creek. But he didn't want to be separated from Juliet, either. It felt like an impossible choice.

Pushing the conflicting thoughts from his mind, he pulled out his cell. "Mind if I make a call?"

"Go for it. Tell your friend I look forward to meeting him."

Nate's steps felt light as he exited the barn, heading out back for some privacy. Shivering in the frigid winter air, he dialed the shelter.

Susan answered after the second ring.

"Hey, Susan! It's Nate." Excitement rippled through him, lending some warmth. "Can you put Dozer on? I have some good news."

Silence filled the speaker, and Nate checked the connection. "Susan?"

Her strange, staccato breath on the other end of the line made his pulse kick up a notch. His skin prickled. "What's wrong?"

"It's Dozer." Her voice strained with barely suppressed tears.

Nate's grip tightened around the phone, his heart frozen on its last beat as the world around him blurred into the background. "What happened?"

"He—he was hit by a car, crossing a busy intersection." Her stilted explanation ended on a small sob.

A sharp pang shot through Nate's chest. The earth swayed. His eyes burning, he leaned his head against the rough wood siding of the barn. *This isn't happening.*

"Witnesses said Dozer appeared intoxicated and he stepped into the street without any warning. The driver swerved, but it didn't make a difference. Dozer—" She sucked in a strangled breath. "He's in critical condition."

Nate's knees buckled, and he sank to the ground.

"I would've called, but the doctors aren't letting anyone but family see him right now."

"We're his family." The gravelly words scraped his raw, swollen throat.

"I know," Susan whispered. After a deafening pause, she added softly, "There isn't anything you could've done, honey. These things happen."

A cold numbness crept over him, like he was slowly sinking in a frozen pond.

"Nate?" Susan prodded, a warble of fear in her voice. "You know this isn't your fault. You did everything you could for Dozer. And the accident... no one could foresee it."

She continued to offer reassurance, but Nate didn't hear a word.

The phone slipped from his grip, tumbling into the frostbitten dirt.

Closing his eyes, he sank deeper into the icy water of grief until the surface closed over him.

He waited for the world to go black.

CHAPTER 27

FRANK

F rank clicked through the TV channels, grumbling to himself. *Dagnabbit.* Christmas programs monopolized every station. Why did he pay for the pricier cable package when every channel played the same thing? Maybe Bevy was right—maybe the whole *streaming* fad was the way to go.

Frustrated by the abysmal selection, he didn't even mind when the landline bellowed, demanding his presence in the kitchen. Maybe it would be a solicitor from the cable company. He'd give him an earful.

"Hello?" he barked.

"Mr. Barrie, it's Susan." The woman sounded so distraught Frank instantly softened.

"What seems to be the trouble?"

"It's Nate. I just got off the phone with him a few minutes ago. I'm afraid I had to give him some bad news."

"What sort of bad news?" The new French roast turned out to be a little bitter kind of bad news? Or an entire crop of Brazilian beans was decimated by coffee berry borers—the bane of every farmer's livelihood—kind of news?

"One of his friends in the shelter was in an accident a few days ago. Someone he was mentoring. He's in critical condition. Nate took it pretty hard."

Drat. The poor kid. The bad news definitely rivaled a coffee borer–level catastrophe. Maybe worse.

"What can I do?"

"Keep an eye on him. Make sure he's okay. He, uh, had an issue a while back. I didn't mention it because it hasn't been a concern for over a year."

"What kind of issue?" Frank's pulse quickened. He didn't like where this conversation was headed.

"Prescription sleeping pills."

Frank scrunched his eyes shut. He was afraid it would be something like that.

"I hate that my thoughts are even going down this road," Susan admitted, sniffling. "I trust Nate. I really do. At least, I want to. But there was something in his voice when we got off the phone. I don't know how to describe it. But it scared me enough to call you."

Frank opened his eyes, his gaze fixed on the hallway leading to his bedroom—where he kept his medications. "Thanks for the call. I'll check on Nate. He's in good hands." He didn't offer her false assurances like Bevy might have. He imagined his wife would say something like, *Don't worry, everything will be fine.* But Frank couldn't promise that.

He wanted to believe in the boy. Private Henderson had given him every reason to trust him explicitly. And yet, tragedy—especially concerning a close friend—could do funny things to a man. It could tie him into knots until up looked like down and down looked like up.

He replaced the receiver and shuffled into their bedroom, heading straight for Bevy's nightstand. She insisted on keeping his sleeping pills on her side, since he apparently couldn't be trusted to take them.

He yanked open the drawer. He'd find the pills and rule out Susan's suspicion. Moving aside Bevy's Bible, an extra pair of reading glasses, and stack of paperbacks, he found several plastic bottles with her name on them, but no sleeping pills.

His heart rate accelerated again, much too fast for a man his age. Maybe Bevy accidentally put them away in his nightstand? He ambled across the room and checked his side of the bed, aggressively rummaging through his belongings with a single-minded focus.

Where were the pills?

He grabbed an orange bottle from the back of the drawer, squinting at the label. Why did they make the font so small?

Heart medication. *Drat.* He flung the bottle over his shoulder onto the bed, and immediately grabbed another one. *No luck.* He checked several more, then jerked the drawer from the nightstand and spilled the contents onto the quilted comforter.

Still no sleeping pills.

He moved the hunt to the bathroom, flinging open every drawer and cupboard willy-nilly, like a burglar in search of priceless jewels.

He had to find the pills somewhere. Because the alternative—that Nate had taken them—simply couldn't be true.

CHAPTER 28

JULIET

Juliet chewed her French-tipped nail, staring at the Send button. Was she really going to risk submitting a romance novel to her editor? She'd respectfully explained the change in direction in the body of the email, begging for Debra to at least read the first few pages of her manuscript before tossing it in the slush pile, where submissions went to die. She'd also included a one-page proposal and a three-page synopsis. She'd stopped short of including the birth rights to her firstborn child, not convinced it would hold much sway with the single workaholic, anyway.

She thought back to Nate's words of encouragement from earlier. He'd given her permission to tell his story. He trusted her. Maybe it was time she trusted herself?

With a deep, shuddering breath, she hit Send. The email jetted into the Ethernet.

She did it! No takesies-backsies.

Now, for the hard part.

She pulled out her cell.

"Hi, sweetheart." Her mother answered on the first ring. She never answered on the first ring.

"Hi, Mom."

"I was just talking about you," her mother purred, sounding cheerful and blissfully unaware her world was about to implode. "You need to come visit me after the holidays. England can be quite dreary in the winter, but you'll love Oxford. It's a literary powerhouse, producing prodigies like Percy Shelley, Oscar Wilde, and Harper Lee. You may even stumble upon some inspiration for your next book."

Juliet's heart twisted. Had her mother actually invited her to visit? She couldn't remember a single time in her life when her mother had requested her presence anywhere. This phone call was going to be even harder than she anticipated.

"There's something I need to tell you." Her fingernail found its way between her teeth again. So much for her manicure.

"What is it, sweetheart?"

"I just sent Debra my manuscript."

"That's fabulous news! We should celebrate. I think I have a bottle of champagne here somewhere."

Muffled noises filled the speaker, and Juliet gazed up at the ceiling, her eyes burning at her mother's unsuspecting happiness. "Mom, wait. Before you get too excited, there's something else you should know."

"What is it?" An edge of caution crept into her mother's voice.

Juliet gathered another breath, exhaling in a single puff. "I didn't submit the novel you and Debra discussed."

"What does that mean?"

"I—I don't want to write literary fiction. At least, not right now."

"I don't understand. If not literary fiction, then what else is there? Nonfiction?"

"Romance." Once the word escaped, Juliet clamped her bottom lip between her teeth, prepared for the worst. She expected her mother would follow the textbook stages of grief, starting with shock and denial, then lingering in anger and bargaining before firmly planting herself in depression. She doubted they'd ever make it to the acceptance stage.

After the longest pause known to mankind—during which Juliet's bottom lip swelled two sizes from her incessant gnawing—her mother asked, "Why?" in an ice-cold whisper.

Juliet shivered. She would've preferred yelling and shouting over the eerie calm before the storm. "I tried to write the kind of book we talked about. Truly, I did. But it just wasn't in me. But this story, the one I sent Debra, flowed out of me, like I'd been holding it inside for far too long. And—" *Keep going. Say everything in your heart. No regrets.* "I think it's good, Mom. With some editing, I think it's publishable. And more than that, I think readers will like it. And that's why I want to write. To connect with readers. To write something that will make other people smile. I know that sounds silly to you. Demeaning, even. A waste of time. But it's what I want to do with my life. And I hope, even if you can't understand it, you'll at least respect my decision." *That you'll respect* me, her heart silently pleaded.

When Juliet finally stopped speaking, she felt like she'd chugged a thousand espressos—wired and exhilarated and, also, bizarrely at peace.

She waited for her mother to unleash her rebuttal, explaining how she'd just made the biggest mistake of her life.

Instead, her mother said the last thing Juliet expected. "I'll withhold further comment until I hear what Debra has to say. But Juliet"—her voice dropped an octave, low and ominous—"I hope you won't live to regret this."

"I won't," Juliet said with a level of confidence that surprised her. If Debra didn't want *A Soldier's Christmas Promise*, she'd query somewhere else. Or publish it herself. She believed in the story too much to give up on it.

And perhaps even more startling, she finally believed in herself. Maybe even enough to bet on herself.

As she hung up the phone, her mind reeled with what-ifs. What if this novel was only the first of many? What if she stayed in Poppy Creek and focused on her writing? She could work remotely for Reclaim, driving into the city for the monthly company-wide meetings. Eventually, she could pare down her hours, as needed. She doubted she'd ever leave the nonprofit completely, but her role could change. She could also donate a percentage of royalties and bring more awareness to the cause through her writing.

Excitement fluttered in her chest at the myriad of thrilling possibilities, of her and Nate staying in the idyllic town together.

A knock at the door drew her attention from her

daydreams. The door creaked open, and Frank poked his head inside. At the look on his face, Juliet's heart stopped cold. She jumped from the chair. "What's wrong?" *Please, don't tell me something happened to Aunt Beverly.*

"Have you seen Nate?"

"Not in a while, why?" Her pulse sputtered.

"I need to find him. I've checked all over the house—"

"Is he with Vick in the barn?" Nate had been hanging out with Vick quite often during her writing sessions.

"Vick's already left for the day. And I checked the barn. No sign of Nate. And his car's gone."

"Frank, what's going on?" There was something he wasn't telling her.

She stood in stunned silence as Frank relayed his phone call with Susan. Her heart ached for what Nate must be going through, but when Frank got to the part about the pills, she stiffened.

"With all due respect, Susan's wrong. Nate told me all about that part of his past, and I know he wouldn't go back there. Not even for something like this."

Frank shuffled his feet, looking even more uncomfortable than before.

"What else aren't you telling me?"

"I take sleeping pills. And I—I can't find them."

At this new piece of information, time seemed to slow down. Her heart thudded loudly inside her chest, pumping adrenaline through her blood at an alarming rate, but she shook her head, adamant in Nate's innocence. "Then there's some other explanation. I know Nate. He didn't take them."

"I want to believe that, too. But I've looked everywhere."

"Then let's look again. I'll help."

As they made their way to Frank and her aunt's bedroom, she asked, "Did you call Nate and ask him?"

"I tried. He didn't answer."

"Poppy Creek doesn't have the greatest cell reception," she said by way of explanation. "Or he could be driving."

Frank merely nodded, but she could see the worry in his eyes. For the next several minutes, they double-checked everywhere Frank had already looked. No sign of the pills anywhere. Juliet wanted to cry in frustration.

"Good heavens, what happened here?" Aunt Beverly stood in the doorway, gaping at the mess.

"We're looking for Frank's sleeping pills," Juliet blurted, searching under the bed for the tenth time. "Have you seen them?"

"Yes, of course. But why do you need them now? It's barely five o'clock."

"Where are they?" Juliet scrambled to her feet, her heart frantic with hope.

"In the kitchen." Aunt Beverly glanced between them, her forehead furrowed in confusion.

"Show me." Juliet barged out of the bedroom, desperate to see the pill bottle with her own eyes, to prove to Frank she'd been right all along.

"I had them in here this morning." Aunt Beverly sifted through a pile of mail by the landline. "Dolores mentioned she was having trouble sleeping, so I said I'd call her with Frank's prescription, so she could ask her doctor about it. Ah. Here it is." She turned and shook the bottle, rattling the pills inside. "Now, what's this all about?"

Juliet flung her arms around her aunt's neck, overwhelmed with relief. "Thank you, thank you."

One crisis averted. But they still needed to find Nate.

Juliet prayed he was okay.

CHAPTER 29

NATE

Nate tensed the instant he crossed the threshold of the kitchen and caught the current of anxiety sizzling through the room. His hands clenched. What now? He couldn't handle any more bad news today. "Is everything okay?" he asked cautiously, not wanting to jump to worst-case scenarios.

"Nate!" Juliet threw herself into his arms, clinging so tightly to his neck, he struggled to breathe. "Thank goodness you're all right."

Holding her close, he darted a curious glance between Frank and Beverly. Had they all been worried about him? He'd been gone an hour, maybe two, *tops*. He hadn't expected anyone to notice his absence, let alone cause alarm. "What's going on?"

"Susan called." Frank's statement said it all.

Of course she did. Nate should've anticipated Susan calling out of concern. She had a big heart and cared deeply. She must've been worried about the way they'd left things earlier. He'd call her soon and let her know he was okay.

"We're so, so sorry about your friend." Juliet tipped her head back, meeting his gaze. Tears of shared grief shimmered in her dark eyes. "I wish there was something we could do."

He held her gaze for a moment, marveling at her depth of compassion. She looked so earnest, so sincere. So did Frank and Beverly. They each wore an expression that mirrored how he'd felt mere hours earlier—helpless yet desperate to do something. "Maybe there is."

"Anything," Juliet said so quickly, he couldn't help but smile. He knew she meant the offer.

"Can we sit? I have something important to share with you all."

"Of course! I'll make some tea." In her gentle, motherly way, Beverly shooed them into the sitting room while she set the kettle on the stove.

A few minutes later, they'd all settled around the fireplace with warm mugs of orange-cinnamon tea in hand. Except for Frank. He seemed mystified by the entire concept of tea, bordering on personally affronted.

Nate sipped the sweet amber liquid, mentally capturing the scene before him. Frank, Beverly, and Juliet—three people he'd known for such a short time but who'd already become like family. The potted Christmas tree by the bay window cast a rainbow glow across their features, lending his mental image a magical effect.

A week ago, he never could've predicted this particular turn of events. He almost couldn't believe how drastically his life had changed.

"What's on your mind?" Juliet asked softly, cradling her tea beside him on the couch.

From their perch on the matching armchairs by the fireplace, Frank and Beverly fixed him with expressions of interest and something deeper, something close to parental care and regard, bordering on tenderness. The realization soothed a splintered fissure of his heart left ragged and razor-sharp for years. A lifetime, even.

Nate took another sip, then set the teacup back on its saucer on the coffee table. "When Susan told me about Dozer, I took the news pretty hard."

Juliet reached for his hand, and he gratefully accepted her offer of comfort. "I felt like I'd let Dozer down. That if I'd done more to help him, he never would've reached for the bottle again, that the accident never would've happened." Nate's throat strained as he swallowed. "True or not, the thought dragged me back into the darkest corners of my mind, the places I swore I'd never revisit. I don't know how long I would've sat on the cold ground, or what I would've done, if Vick hadn't found me."

A fresh wave of gratitude surged in his chest, tightening his throat another notch. "We talked about how hard it is for vets to come home, the struggle to reassimilate, to find a new sense of purpose. Vick shared how working with you changed his life." He met Frank's gaze. The man's features remained unreadable, but his eyes—steel gray and stormy—glinted with emotion.

"I started thinking about Luke's job offer and what it would mean for my life." He squeezed Juliet's hand, offering her unspoken assurances. He hadn't told her his final decision yet, and he prayed she would understand.

She squeezed back, as if offering her own reassurance in return.

"We realized we both were given an opportunity many vets never receive—a chance to start over with a solid support system in place. And we wondered what it would look like to help more vets get a similar second chance."

"And did you think of something?" Beverly leaned forward, the teacup in her lap long forgotten.

"We did." Nate traced his thumb in a circle over the back of Juliet's hand as he met her gaze again. Her dark eyes locked with his, warm and soft, waiting for him to continue with an openness and acceptance that renewed his resolve. "We're calling it the SP Project. The acronym stands for Soldier's Promise."

A spark of surprise flickered in Juliet's eyes, then tears welled as she made the connection between the name they'd chosen and the title of her novel, just like he'd hoped she would.

"We plan to run a trade school program here in Poppy Creek. For three to six months, depending on the time needed, a vet will live in town and learn a new trade. They'll not only receive valuable training, gaining skills that will help transition them into a new career, but they'll be brought into the community, too. Luke already agreed to be the beta test. And Cassie said she could offer business management training and thinks Eliza would agree to a baking apprenticeship. She also plans to bring up the proposal at the next town hall meeting to see who else is interested in participating." Nate's heart warmed at how readily Luke and Cassie jumped on board the idea, wanting to help in whatever way possible. Cassie even suggested her friend Kat might be willing to host a vet at the inn she owns during the program. Although it was a generous offer, Nate would feel better if he could raise donations to supplement the cost.

"We obviously have a lot of details to sort out," he added. "But we're hopeful. Turns out, Vick has been thinking about this for a while. Frank, he'd even planned to ask you if he could set something up at the roastery."

Frank's eyes widened at the news, but Nate still couldn't tell what he thought of the idea. Nate cleared his throat. "Vick wanted to hold off until he had more of the details figured out. His concept really caught fire as we talked and were able to bounce ideas off each other. Then, with Luke and Cassie involved, more of the pieces fell into place." Nate's pulse quickened as he recalled the spirited exchange of ideas, everyone's excitement growing as the plan took shape.

"We thought Susan could make nominations for participants from the shelter when she thinks someone is ready for the program. Then there's the legwork necessary to get them set up with a job once they complete their training, but we have time to flesh out the specifics." More than anything, he wanted Dozer to be the first trainee. He needed to believe his friend would recover, that this wasn't the end. "Vick and I will iron out the wrinkles over the next several weeks and hopefully have a streamlined proposal early next year." Nate paused to gather a breath. He'd been talking for several minutes straight. Had his heart been pounding this loudly the entire time?

Reeling with adrenaline and nervous energy, he glanced around the room, realizing how desperately he desired their approval. His throat suddenly dry, he asked, "So, what do you think?"

"I think it's a lovely idea." Beverly beamed like a chuffed mama hen, her palm pressed to her chest as if her heart might burst.

Although pleased by her reaction, Nate wouldn't celebrate just yet. He looked at Juliet, his blood pumping overtime. He needed her to know how much she'd inspired him. "Something you said in your novel really stuck with me. About how your character found God's love reflected in the kindness of others, like the brightest star in the sky guiding him to where he belonged."

A tearful smile spread across her face. "You remembered?"

"I'll never forget." He returned her smile, warmth washing over him. "We have this expression in the service: no man left behind. It's a promise to live by. But being here, meeting you, taught me that promise extends beyond the military. We should all be there for one another, doing life together, supporting each other in every way we can. We're stronger when we're in community. And I've seen that truth lived out, here, in Poppy Creek." He wanted to tell her he planned to stay and that he'd do whatever it took to make things work between them. But before he had a chance, she leaned forward and kissed him, oblivious to their audience.

When their lips parted, she was still smiling through her tears. "I love this idea, Nate. Almost as much as I love you."

Her words crashed into him like a cleansing wave, chipping away at every whispered self-doubt telling him he wasn't worthy of love. His eyes burned white-hot. With a sharp breath, he closed them, pressing his forehead to hers. "I love you, too, Jules." His heart ached with happiness as he tilted her chin, bringing her lips to his once more.

A throat cleared, yanking his attention to their lack of privacy.

They broke apart, flushed and sheepish.

Beverly clasped her hands together in blissful delight, as if she'd just glimpsed Santa Claus himself. Juliet blushed, her dark eyes glowing. Frank, on the other hand, had an impeccable poker face.

Nate would give anything to read the man's thoughts. Frank's opinion—and approval—meant more to him than he'd realized.

All eyes turned to Frank as he sat in silence, stewing.

Finally, after what felt like an eternity and a half, Frank met his gaze. "I'm proud of you, son." The words rang clear and strong, without a single grunt or growl. For the first time in his life, Nate felt something stir deep in his gut. Something he'd formerly revered as forever beyond his reach. The elusive, indescribable, incomparable weight of a father's love.

The rest of the evening, they talked more about the trade school, brainstorming over a fresh pot of coffee and leftover pie and finger foods in lieu of dinner.

When Frank and Beverly excused themselves for bed, Nate and Juliet remained snuggled on the couch, gazing into the smoldering embers of the dwindling fire.

Twirling her loose tendril around his finger, he told her, "I know me staying here isn't ideal, but we'll still see each other all the time. I plan to visit Dozer in the hospital as soon as possible. Then I can come down on weekends, whatever it takes to make this work when you go back home."

She looked up at him with a mischievous twinkle in her eyes. "What do you mean? I'm already home."

EPILOGUE

FRANK

Frank stood in the doorway between the kitchen and sitting room, mobbed on either side by hordes of people. And not just *people*. People clad in the ugliest sweaters he'd ever seen. Bevy had made him wear one, too. Itchy wool appliquéd with a snowman drinking hot chocolate. Wouldn't hot chocolate melt a snowman? Essentially, she'd made him wear a macabre murder scene. Death by hot chocolate. Not that she'd listened when he pointed out that factoid. It's all part of the fun, she'd said, while explaining the peculiar concept of an Ugly Christmas Sweater party.

She used the expression a lot, he'd come to realize. *It's all part of the fun.* The other part of the equation usually involved some sort of personal sacrifice, like stuffing his house shoulder to shoulder with houseguests. But he shouldn't complain. At least he liked most of them.

He glanced back into the kitchen. Bevy loaded a serving dish with the tiniest sandwiches known to man, and Eliza slid another tray of fragrant gingersnap cookies from the oven. Nate and Juliet sat at the small dining table, wishing her parents a merry Christmas through her laptop screen. FaceTime, they called it. Which he supposed made sense, since that's about all you saw of the person on the flat screen.

This is the second time Juliet had made one of these video calls to her parents during the last few weeks. The previous time, she'd announced her revised book deal. Her current editor hadn't wanted to take on the romance novel herself, but she'd passed it off to a colleague at the same publishing house, who'd loved it. Now Juliet had a two-book contract for *A Soldier's Christmas Promise* and an unnamed sequel. Juliet's father—who struck Frank as an oddly emotional fellow—had been thrilled by the news, claiming his daughter "spoke the language of romance in her soul," whatever that mumbo jumbo meant. Juliet's mother, however, was still warming up to the change in direction. Although, she did seem to like Nate, so Juliet said she'd take the win.

Frank knew these things because Juliet had plenty of time to fill him in over their morning coffee now that she'd moved in with them. Yep. That's right. He lived with two chatty females. At least most of the time they talked to each other. Or Nate. He'd moved into a studio apartment above the antiques shop on Main Street, and ate most of his meals with them, which Bevy loved. She'd always wanted kids of her own, and now that she'd gotten her wish, they had two extra mouths to feed. He pretended to complain, but he couldn't fool a smart cookie like his Bevy. She knew he secretly liked having them around.

He'd become the silent benefactor of Nate and Vick's

SP Project, grateful to put more of his bank account to good use. Or more importantly, to finally answer the quiet yearning in his heart to do more for service members in need. Service members like Dozer.

Nate's friend had made a turn for the better, and although he'd need more time in recovery, he seemed eager to roast under Vick's tutelage, once the doctors gave him the green light.

Frank couldn't be more proud of Vick. Or Nate. Odd how he'd welcomed the boy into his home as a gift to Bevy, but in the end, Frank may have benefitted even more than his wife. Not that he'd admit that tidbit to anyone but himself. If he did, Bevy might invite the entire shelter into their home. And they didn't have enough cots for that.

Glancing back into the sitting room, Frank glimpsed Bevy's hospitable spirit firsthand. Based on the festive throng, she'd invited everyone in town, including one or two guests of the nonhuman variety. Most notably, Bill Tucker's pet pig, Peggy Sue, who appeared to be enjoying her own plate of hors d'oeuvres.

"You don't have to stand there all day. If you want a kiss, all you have to do is ask." Bevy sidled up beside him, her teasing smile brightening her blue eyes.

Frank glanced overhead. A sprig of mistletoe hung from the doorjamb above them. Another holiday custom he didn't understand. Why not tack poison ivy around the house, too? Well, at least he got a kiss out of the hair-brained tradition. Much more pleasant than an itchy sweater.

Careful not to spill her tray of tiny sandwiches, he bent

and kissed his wife. In that brief moment, all the noise and chaos melted away.

When the kiss ended, she didn't go back to the party like he'd expected. She set the tray on the credenza, just outside the doorway, then wrapped both arms around his waist. Bing Crosby's classic "Jingle Bells" emanated from the record player.

Frank waited for his muscles to tense at the all-too-familiar tune, but they didn't. Instead, he relaxed as Bevy snuggled in closer.

Cassie, who cradled her daughter, Edie, on the couch, started singing along to the song, then Luke joined her. Before long, the entire sitting room reverberated with the joyful sound of harmonized voices.

Bevy leaned her head against his shoulder. "This has been the best Christmas ever," she whispered. "Thank you, darling."

Too overcome with emotion to speak, he planted a kiss on his wife's head, savoring the single most perfect moment in his life.

Maybe "Jingle Bells" wasn't so bad after all.

If you enjoyed A Very Barrie Christmas, you'll also enjoy Blessings on State Street.

Grieving widow Abigail Preston wants nothing to do with Christmas this year. When she discovers her late husband owned a waterfront home in the quaint, cozy community of Blessings Bay, she figures it's the perfect holiday hideout. Except, there's one problem: An unexpected—and distractingly handsome—houseguest.

ACKNOWLEDGMENTS

It's time to thank our usual suspects.

First, all my love and thanks to my incredible family for their unwavering support. They never hesitate to lend a hand, whether I need someone to watch Violet for a few hours or I have a plot question.

I'm also eternally grateful for my amazing team, from my cover designer, Ana Grigoriu-Voicu with Books-Design, to the dynamic editing duo, Krista Dapkey and Beth Attwood.

The humblest thanks to my critique partners, Dawn Malone and Elizabeth Bråten, for their writerly instincts and insights.

And continued thanks to my lovely team of early readers. I appreciate you all more than I can say!

Last but not least, heartfelt thanks and hugs to you, dear reader. I never thought this series would reach 9 books, and you're still asking for more. That's the greatest gift I could hope for. Thank you!

ABOUT THE AUTHOR

Rachael Bloome is a *USA Today* bestselling author of contemporary romance and women's fiction novels featuring hope, healing, and the unbreakable bonds of found family.

Rachael is a hope*ful* romantic joyfully living in her very own love story. She's passionate about her faith, family, friends, and her French press. When she's not writing, helping to run the family coffee roasting business, or getting together with friends, she's busy planning their next big adventure.

Learn more about Rachael and her uplifting love stories at www.rachaelbloome.com and connect via the following social media sites (you can even listen to free audiobooks on her YouTube channel!):

ALSO BY RACHAEL BLOOME

BLESSINGS BAY SERIES

Blessings on State Street

The Unexpected Inn

The Unbound Bookshop

The Uncomplicated Café

STANDALONE NOVELS

New York, New Year, New You

BOOK CLUB QUESTIONS

1. Nate is an unusual hero due to his unglamorous past. What did you think of his character? Did you find him to be a worthy romance hero? Why or why not?

2. Juliet's desire to meet her parents' expectations heavily influenced her career. Do you think this is a common issue young adults face? What advice would you give someone in Juliet's shoes?

3. Nate tells Juliet, "There's no such thing as just a romance novel. Books are special. They can evoke any number of emotions, from anger to outrage, grief and empathy, even joy. Especially joy." Do you agree with this statement? What do you think makes books special?

4. When Nate tells Juliet about kintsugi—the Japanese art of repairing broken objects with gold—he says the tradition serves as a reminder that "God not only makes broken things beautiful, He gives them a purpose. And part of that purpose is to share our story, our scars, so others know healing and restoration is possible." Do you agree with this perspective? Why or why not?

5. Juliet abandons her literary novel aspirations to write a romance novel instead. Do you agree with this decision? Or do you think she should've stuck to her original book proposal?

6. According to recent statistics, veterans are more likely to experience homelessness than non-veterans. What did you think

of Vick and Nate's trade school project for veterans? What other solutions can you think of to help combat the issue?

7. Frank stepped outside his comfort zone to help give Beverly the best Christmas ever. In what ways have you had to sacrifice during the holidays for the sake of others? Did it bring you unexpected blessings?

8. In Juliet's novel, she wrote this about her character, Nick: He'd come to the small town of Thistle River in search of a light bright enough to dim the darkness inside him.He thought he'd find it among the festive trappings and trimmings, but he'd looked in all the wrong places. In the end, Nick found God's love reflected in the kindness of others. Where do you see God's love and the spirit of Christmas during the holidays?

9. Vick tells Nate that gratitude and positive thoughts are important, but there's also great power in community, "the kind of family you forge one friendship at a time." Do you agree with this statement?

10. What do you think is the theme of the novel?

As always, I look forward to hearing your thoughts on the story. You can email your responses (or ask your own questions) to hello@rachaelbloome.com or post them in my private Facebook group, Rachael Bloome's Secret Garden Book Club.

BEVERLY'S PERFECT PIE CRUST RECIPE

INGREDIENTS

2 1/2 cups all-purpose flour

1 teaspoon kosher salt or 1/2 teaspoon fine sea salt

1 tablespoon sugar

1 cup frozen unsalted butter, grated

6-8 tablespoons ice water, or more as needed

INSTRUCTIONS

1. Grate two sticks of frozen butter into a bowl and place in the freezer for 15 minutes.

2. Measure the flour using a scale or fluff with a fork, spoon into a measuring cup, then level with a flat edge.

3. Add flour, salt, and sugar to a medium bowl. Stir to combine.

4. Add grated butter and combine with a fork. Dough will be crumbly.

5. Slowly add ice water, adding as little water as necessary until the dough comes together.

5. Shape into two mounds, wrap in plastic wrap, and place in the refrigerator for 2 hours up to overnight.

6. Remove dough from the refrigerator and allow to sit at room temperature for 5 minutes.

7. On a lightly floured surface, roll each mound of dough into a

12-in circle (about 1/8-inch thick).

8. Gently press one circle into a pie dish, then place in the freezer for 5 minutes.

9. Remove from freezer, fill pie crust with desire filling, then top with the second circle of dough.

10. Trim and crimp edges. Cut vents in the top of the crust, then place back in the freezer for 5 minutes.

11. Bake according to pie instructions.

Enjoy!

A Very Barrie Christmas Party

Frank & Beverly Barrie hosted a festive holiday party, inviting guests to don their ugliest Christmas sweaters. Luke Davis dressed as Santa Claus and gave gifts to the children. Colt Davis and Jack Gardener added to the fun with a 2-person reindeer costume. However, in a comical mixup, they each arrived wearing the back end of the reindeer.

As a Plan B, Jack's husky, Fitz, wore reindeer antlers along with Bill Tucker's pet pig, Peggy Sue. Dolores Whittaker tried to include her burly tabby cat, Banjo, in the sleigh-pulling ensemble, but he staunchly refused, looking down on his counterparts with pity and thinly veiled disdain. The children were delighted by the display.

Home for the Holidays

In a moving speech at the Christmas Eve Dance, Mayor Davis welcomed two new residents to Poppy Creek, Nate Henderson and Juliet Klein.

In closing, Davis extolled, "May our town forever be a welcoming beacon to those looking for a place to call home. And may we always have room for one more, in our community and in our hearts."

From our family to yours, *Merry Christmas!*

Made in the USA
Las Vegas, NV
19 December 2024

14887923R00111